FEAR THE FALL

MELISSA WINTERS

This is a work of fiction. All of the characters and events portrayed in this novel are products of the author's imagination. Any resemblance to actual persons or businesses is unintentional.

No part of this book may be reproduced in any form or by any electronic or mechanical means, including information storage and retrieval systems, without written permission from the author, except for the use of brief quotations in a book review.

Copyright © 2020 by Melissa Winters

All rights reserved.

Edited by Per Se Editing

Cover Design by: Regina Wamba of ReginaWamba.com.

Fear The Fall Playlist

The Night We Met by Lord Huron
Radioactive by Imagine Dragons
Monsters by All Time Low
Miracle by The Score
Redemption by Besomorph & Coopex
Play with Fire by Sam Tinnesz
Believer by Imagine Dragons
Riptide by Vance Joy
Wolves by Missio
Something Just Like This by The Chainsmokers & Coldplay
Stay by Rihanna
Sucker for Pain by Lil Wayne, Wiz Khalifa & Imagine Dragons
Bad Blood by Taylor Swift
You're Somebody Else by Flora Cash
Therefore I Am by Billie Eilish
Devil Devil by Milck
First by Cold War Kids
Help by Papa Roach
Hell Froze Over by Kodaline
Blame by Bastille
Everybody Rise by Amy Shark
Dead Inside by Muse
Bloody Valentine by Machine Gun Kelly
Chop Suey! by System of A Down
Helium by Sia

This book is for my friend Mary Donovan for all the times I've asked her to read my books for proofing errors and mistakes. She drops everything to help and she'll never know how much I love and appreciate her! This one's for you girl!

"Once upon a time, an angel and a devil fell in love. It did not end well."
—Laini Taylor

PROLOGUE

THE NIGHT WE MET

A PAIR of sea-green eyes meet mine and time stops.

It doesn't matter that a lady is bleeding out at my knees, a casualty in a fight with a legion of demons. I'm transfixed by the man holding the woman in his arms. His five o'clock shadow and ruffled light brown hair make him look rugged and masculine. Not things I should be noticing, considering the woman is dying and I should be long gone by now.

"Can you help her?" he yells, over the wail of demons being dragged to hell.

If not for the fact that he's looking right at me, I'd think he was just calling out for help, because humans aren't supposed to see angels unless God wills it so.

"Help her." His eyes plead with me.

I jerk backward. "You can see me?"

"Yes, I can see you. Are you going to help?"

I shake the stupor away, baffled by the fact that this human can in fact see me. That's not possible, unless something has changed. It happens very rarely, but there have been a couple of occasions where God has given his divine mercy at the last second. I don't question God's choices.

He's speaking to me, and that can't be good for him.

Witnessing a holy war will sign this man's death warrant.

It's law. Humans can't be privy to knowledge of our kind. They're to have faith in our existence, but signs are forbidden —except through miracles that I, as a virtue angel, can provide. Typically, sightings are cause for cleanup of the extermination variety. Humans aren't to be touched unless they threaten the balance, and his being able to see me disrupts the balance in an epic way.

"How can you see me?" I demand, looking for some sign that this is, in fact, God's will.

"I don't have those answers, angel. Can you help her?" he repeats a little more forcefully.

I shake my head. "I can't," I whisper, feeling as though I'm betraying a man I don't even know, from the way he frowns in my direction. The look of disappointment sears through me.

It's not my place to interfere in a human's fate. I'm not to have interaction with humans, let alone save one. By law, I should end his life and the woman's right now, or at the very least, call for an angel of death to do the dirty work. Or I could provide a miracle and hope God approves of an unsanctioned one.

"Please," the man begs. "She's a mother. If you won't do it for me, do it for her three kids."

I run my hands down my face, feeling a rush of cold that I shouldn't feel. Angels don't experience such things. The elements don't affect us, and I certainly can't care about this woman's family.

But for some reason, I do.

"Is she your wife?" The words slip past my mouth before I can stop them.

The less I know, the better. Being on Earth is horrifically hard for angels, as we don't typically experience the range of emotions that humans do. Here, I'm getting caught up in matters that don't concern me.

"No. She's just an innocent bystander who got stuck in the cross fire."

I bite my lip, thinking over the options.

The man's hand lies atop mine, and shivers course through me.

"Help her."

"Why do you want to help her?" I don't know why I ask. It doesn't matter and it won't change anything.

"She doesn't deserve to die for being in the wrong place at the wrong time. Surely you agree?"

His eyes pierce mine; the weight of his words weighs heavily on me. Without another thought, I place my hands on her chest and allow the energy I've stored to flow through me into her, shocking life back into her body. She inhales sharply, indicating I've just fucked up royally.

If any of my brothers witnessed this, I'd be summoned to the Divine Council. Since it's my first offense, I'll beg for clemency and swear fealty to my legion. A lifetime's worth of battle cleanup might save me. Or I'll be stripped of my wings and barred from Heaven—a fate worse than death. Either option is horrific to consider. And for what? A bit of human lust? That's what this was, right?

How a virtue angel was able to be affected by such things is a question I'll need to mull over in greater detail once I'm far away from here and this devastatingly handsome mortal. I'm one of the strongest beings. Even if Earth affects angels, it shouldn't affect a virtue this much. I cringe at the thought. The weakness seeps into my being, making me feel dirty and traitorous.

"She'll survive," I say, knowing I need to leave immediately. Something in the air is off.

The sirens blaring in the background indicate that more humans are on their way. It won't be long before quite the scene rains down on me. Glancing around, I'm relieved to see the cleanup process is complete. When the humans get here, they'll find nothing more than an injured woman and a man caring for her. My work is done.

"Wait," he says, reaching out and grabbing my elbow.

A slow burn starts deep in my belly, building all the way up my chest. I close my eyes and attempt to shake off the sensations. Wrong, yet so right.

Emotions like this are impossible for a virtue angel to feel, yet the heat from his touch still burns my skin. Something forbidden. Something that calls to my soul and threatens to rip away my very existence.

"What you saw," I start, and then stop, knowing that what I'm about to say will go against every law of my kind. But when I look back up to his handsome face, I know I have to warn him. "You're in grave danger."

His answering grin confuses me, and I narrow my eyes. He can't be making light of this. Does he not realize that by law, I should kill him on the spot? Does he not know that there is still a real chance that once I leave, another of my brothers could sweep in and do the job I'm somehow incapable—for the first time in my existence—of doing?

"Angel," he says softly. The very words caress my skin. If I were standing, they would surely buckle my traitorously weak knees. He leans over, trailing one finger down my cheek and over the curve of my exposed neck. I shudder under his touch, my eyes closing of their own volition.

"You're in danger," I repeat, stressing the words, needing him to understand the seriousness of this moment.

He shakes his head. "I am the danger."

Something about the way he says it sends goose bumps racing up and down my spine in equal parts intrigue and trepidation. I rush to explain, knowing my time is running out.

"You can never repeat what you've seen here. I won't compel you to forget, but you must never speak a word of this." I stand and turn to go, but he's right behind me, grabbing my elbow once more.

"Why?" he questions, eyes mere slits as he watches me, waiting for my answer. But I don't know what he's asking.

"Why won't you compel me?" he says, solving my unanswered question.

It's such a loaded question. Why indeed? I've been

pondering the same thing this entire time, but it all comes down to one very peculiar thing.

"I can't," I admit, lowering my head.

Something inside me won't allow it. It's not divine intervention. No, this decision is all my own.

"What's your name?"

I sigh. "I can't tell you that."

Giving a human my name is one of the greatest crimes against Heaven. Our names are sacred, given to us by our creator. I took an oath to protect it at all costs, because my name can be used as a weapon against me. Those who speak it can call on me at any moment, and in the hands of a human, that's dangerous.

"What's your name?" he repeats, looking deep into my eyes, burning his features into my memory. Prominent square jaw, sloped nose that gives way to full lips and a slight hollow in his chin. Penetrating green eyes that I'll never forget.

"Victoria," it slips from my lips, unbidden.

He nods, smiling. "Until we meet again, Victoria."

RADIOACTIVE

The clouds roll through, black and ominous. Thunder rumbles in the distance, and for a moment I consider abandoning my post to watch from the shelter of the barn. But that wouldn't be wise. I draw my strength from the energy produced by such storms. The closer I am, the more power I can harness, and I will need it.

Tonight, I hunt.

The thunder booms as the storm moves closer. The wind begins its shrill howl, slicing through the trees. Branches tremble at its force. The promise of destruction comes with every gust.

It won't be long.

A twinge of excitement courses through me at the prospect. I throw my head back, inhaling the fresh air as it caresses my skin. It's then that the sky opens up, bathing me with cool drops of heaven's tears. I cry out as the vortex of energy swirls around me. The warming begins in my toes and I sigh as it crawls up my body, every hair electrified by the energy's touch.

A human could not withstand such a process. Their minds have been closed off from the day of their birth. If they only knew the power they could wield, they'd be unstoppable. The mind is an extraordinary tool capable of anything, but humans rarely tap into that power. Instead, they live their lives defenseless and weak, unable to protect themselves from the evil that surrounds them.

Luckily for me, I am no human. Fallen from grace, I roam the earth determined to earn back my place in the heavens. Stripped of my standing and banished, I now walk amongst Heaven's greatest enemies—demons.

Lightning flashes overhead, pinning me to this spot. Sparks erupt from my hands and I cry out at the exquisite pain. As quickly as the storm began, it's over. The energy recedes, leaving me powerful yet hollow. As a virtue angel, I controlled the elements, and I've somehow carried that gift here to Earth. During storms is the only time I can come close to feeling like I did in Heaven, and it's an effective slap in the face.

I fall to my knees, allowing the residual energy to create spasms throughout my body. Soon all of it will be soaked into my skin and stored for use. I begin to pray—a force of habit I've yet to break. My words are useless. God is undoubtedly not listening.

"Victoria?" I raise my head to a fellow fallen, Ezekiel. "Are you ready?" he asks, voice quiet as he realizes what I'm doing.

I stand to my feet, brushing off the dirt that coats my knees. "I told you, I work alone now."

Two years ago, it was always him by my side. We'd fight together every night and wake up next to each other every morning. Those days ended the moment I realized Zeke was my Band-Aid.

He saved me from crippling despair and helped mold me into what I am today. For that, I owe him my life. But it's not my life he wants. No, that would be my heart, and that was stolen from me.

"It's dangerous, Tori. Why must you be so stubborn?" he practically growls, bringing me back to the present. It's nothing new. We've had this same argument no less than twice per week for the past two years. Since the day I gave him my virginity. Yet he still persists.

"It's not stubbornness; I just don't need you slowing me down," I say, turning my back to one of God's finest creations. He's a work of art, there's no doubt, and that is exactly why I don't need to be anywhere near Ezekiel Kincaid.

I don't trust myself around him. I've already been weak in his presence, and I don't intend to be that person again. He helped me through a trying time, but now I need to help myself.

Then there's the fact that he's teamed up with a few mortals who also hunt demons. Early on, they almost got us killed, because Zeke isn't honest with them. They don't know who or what he really is. He hides his true power. A power he too brought from Heaven. That's a gift that shouldn't be hidden, so I refuse to hunt with them. Why delay the monsters' deaths just to deceive humans?

He barks a laugh. "I'm the best hunter on Earth. It's you who can't keep up with me." My eyes meet his, and the sexy grin he has plastered all over his face makes my insides lava. I push down the lustful feelings, determined to resist.

He's a test and I will not fail. Not this time.

"I'll let you believe what you want to, but as for me, I go alone." As I walk past him, his hand shoots out, grabbing me by the elbow.

"The easiest way to get yourself killed, Tori. I'm just trying to help. Why won't you let anyone help?"

Tearing my arm free, I spin to look right into his cobalt blue eyes. "Because I have a job to do, and your help comes with ulterior motives. You want something we once had, and that's no longer on the table."

"Such as?" he drawls.

"Such as," I repeat snippily, "sex."

His brows rise and his lip quirks in a sexy-as-sin smirk. "Sex?"

"That's what I said."

"You know cuddling is just as good. Maybe a little makeout session." He shrugs. "It doesn't have to necessarily be sex, Tori. I'm open to all forms of foreplay."

"Ugh. See?" I groan. "That's exactly what I'm talking about, Zeke. Unlike you, I don't want to be here," I nearly spit. "I want to go home, and in order to do that, I need to prove my loyalty and allegiance. Falling back into old habits won't get me there."

"I remember a time when you enjoyed those habits."

I did. Zeke was passionate. He took his time and always made sure I was content. He provided comfort in a world that was foreign. I was lonely and he was good company. More importantly, he mended my shattered heart and battered ego. For a short time, at least.

"Yes. I did. Until I finally got my head on straight and my priorities in line."

He scoffs. "You strive for the impossible. No one has ever been allowed back through the gates, and you know that. Once you're forsaken, it's done." His eyes nearly beg me to heed his words.

I continue walking toward the barn, trying to put some distance between us. I've closed the door for us to be more because we have two entirely different paths. I want back in, and he's determined to stay on Earth. He'd be my temptation and the very reason I'd never get home. I've tried to convince him, but he's unmovable in his resolve. Which begs the question . . . why? What is he running from? I don't ask, because that would mean I'd have to share my own past. For two years that's been the one topic of conversation off limits. I don't ask him why he fell, and he doesn't ask me.

"One of these days you're going to admit I'm right," he shouts, but I pay him no mind. "You'll spend a lonely existence until then."

"Good," I call over my shoulder. "Alone is what I need. Alone is what's best. Maybe you should ditch your human shields and use your power to its fullest."

"I'm no fool, Tori. I take help where I can get it. They're safer with me on their team."

"You'll get them killed," I shoot back in frustration. "What will God think then?"

"Nobody is watching, Tori. We're on our own where He's concerned." He doesn't need to clarify who *He* is. "Move on with your life. Embrace Earth. It holds plenty of its own perks."

I whip around, stalking back toward Zeke. "If that's true, then why do you insist on hunting?" I ask, folding my arms over my chest when I'm mere inches from him. "Why not go about your life?" I raise a brow, waiting for his answer.

I'm tired of him constantly questioning me. His actions make less sense. He doesn't want back in Heaven, but he can't help but continue God's work here. It doesn't add up. It never has. Yet another reason to add to my growing list of why I need to stay far away from Zeke. If he'd allow it.

"I'm a hunter, Tori. A power angel. When evil presents itself, I'm called."

"Tsk tsk," I say, waving my fingers in front of his face. "You're a *forsaken* power angel. According to your own words, you're no longer needed. Nobody's watching, so who are you trying to impress, Zeke?"

His hands are at either side of his temples, massaging out the headache I've certainly given him. This is our thing. Fight in circles, getting nowhere. "Maybe I don't like to see God's creation destroyed by those beasts," he shrugs. "All of the perks of Earth depend on Earth's existence. Someone has to save the humans from vampires."

I sigh. "If it's not the vampires, it'll be another form of demon, Zeke. You can't stop them from coming. Lucifer will send legion after legion until this world is destroyed."

But not until he's done toying with humanity—and other beings.

"If you truly have no intention of trying to get back to Heaven, then why not just throw in the towel and enjoy what time is left?" I ask, not understanding why he's committed so much time fighting for a god he chose not to serve. I know little about why he fell, but he has admitted it was his choice. God did not cast him out.

"I've made it my mission to slow down his progress. Like I said, I kinda like Earth, and since I'm immortal and all, I might as well do something of significance."

"You're only immortal until Lucifer finds your weakness. None of us are truly immortal, Zeke. All of our existences can be ended."

"If we work together, we'll have a better chance of survival," he says, leaning forward and taking a piece of my errant hair between his fingers. "We could both enjoy those perks."

I inhale, breathing in the smell of sandalwood and wet earth, my eyes closing to hide the fact that it affects me. He affects me.

"Tori, look at me," he commands, voice husky with want.

I do as he instructs, eyes roaming the six-foot-three warrior. He's tanned and toned everywhere. The muscles in his arms bulge under his white Henley shirt. In the years I've been in this area, I've never seen him do a single thing aside from hunt, and it shows.

"Why did you fall, Zeke?" I whisper.

My hair falls from his grasp as he steps back, running his hands through his raven hair.

"You and I both know that's not a conversation we want to have. When you're ready to share, then I'll consider doing the same."

I sigh, knowing he's right. I haven't uttered a word of why I fell since the day it happened, and I have no intention to. Ever. The shame plagues me daily, and the nightmare of it all haunts my dreams.

"You have to open up to someone, Tori, and I'm all you've got. For reasons I don't understand, we were brought together, and you can't deny it."

"It was a chance encounter," I say, averting my eyes. "And I've been trying to escape you ever since."

"I found you at your lowest point. It was fate."

"You don't believe in fate. It was a simple right place, right time scenario, Zeke."

Completely ignoring my words, he goes on. "Once, I thought you'd share everything with me. You freaked out and I don't understand why."

He knows. I've told him several times a day. Because I want back into Heaven. God is love personified. In his presence, you don't feel things like hate and anger. Here, you feel everything, and it can be painful. Why would anyone choose that? For something like human love? No, thank you.

"You know there are more fallen here on Earth," I say, pumping as much exasperation as possible into my voice. "There have to be. Go find them."

"There aren't," he says, sounding annoyed.

"Perhaps the other fallen are doing exactly what you suggested and enjoying all of Earth's pleasures," I mock, rolling my eyes as I say it.

He grins, moving forward and invading my personal space. I back up, caught off guard by his sudden movement. "There are a lot of pleasures, Tori. Let me remind you. Like old times," he says seductively, leaning into me, inches from my mouth.

I trip backward slightly. "Knock it off, Zeke."

He shoves his hands into his jean pockets and rocks back and forth on his feet. "Ah, come on, Tori, lighten up. It's going to be a long life if you can't have a little fun."

"The only fun I need is slicing my sword into the heart of a vampire," I growl.

I'm frustrated by how much power he has over me. I hate what he makes me want. Makes me crave. He doesn't need to remind me of anything. I remember it all in great detail. The way his hands roamed over my body. His demanding tongue dancing with my own. The way he felt inside of me. I shiver at the thought.

Zeke's phone rings, and he pulls it out from his back pocket. "What?" he barks. His eyes narrow. "Where? . . . I'll be there," he says, before disconnecting the call and placing his phone back into his jeans. "Vamps just outside of Jackson Square."

They're getting braver, coming out earlier and practically in the heart of New Orleans. Rage sweeps through me, the need to unleash the energy trapped inside coursing its way up my spine. It needs to be released.

"Are you coming?" Zeke asks, sounding far too hopeful.

I want to. I miss the days when we fought together, but falling back into our old routines is a recipe for disaster. Zeke doesn't deserve to be my crutch. That's what he was in the beginning, and that's what he'd be now. There's no sense in trying to deny it.

"No. Like I said, I don't fight alongside humans."

His eyes narrow. "If I ditch the humans, will you fight beside me?"

"Get rid of them first, and then we'll talk."

He grins, nodding in satisfaction. "I'll be back," he promises, before turning and jogging off to join the fight.

I have no intention of fighting with him. With or without the humans, my words still stand. I need to do this alone, and Zeke would only complicate things. Getting back to Heaven is my greatest goal, and staying the course is imperative. Angels aren't supposed to enjoy the perks of Earth. They're not meant to dabble in human emotions and pleasure.

Zeke surely does, and that can't have him in God's good graces. Battling demons or not, you don't turn your back on God and get a pass. I'm hoping that atoning in more ways than one will convince Him to give me a second chance. The truth that nobody knows is that I fell to Earth for an angel—one who deceived me.

MONSTERS

My leather-clad leg kicks out as I twist in the air, slamming my steel-toed boot into the back of a demon's head. It hardly registers the impact, shaking off the hit with a simple sneer in my direction. I land on my knees, fist to the ground, ready for the next attack.

I'm outnumbered three to one, but this isn't the worst position I've found myself in. On a typical Friday night, I'm lucky to not find myself smack in the middle of a dozen demons, frothing at the mouth to taste my blood. I might be immortal, but I bleed just like any human, and these creatures crave it.

Despite all the movies and books that romanticize vampires, they're grotesque. Vile doesn't even come close to describing the three disfigured demons in front of me. No two are alike, having been molded into a foul version of their former selves by the torture they earned in Hell. Closer to animal than human, they only slink around in the dark shadows, unable to go unnoticed in the streets of New Orleans.

The city itself breeds evil, but the residents and tourists have no idea how evil. Luckily for them, I have built-in demon radar. If I'm within ten miles of demons, I can track them. And I do. Nightly.

"I'm going to enjoy draining your blood," he jeers, moving toward me with his two buddies flanking him on either side. "It smells"—he sniffs the air with his pig-like snout—"divine."

I titter. "You could even say it's celestial."

He growls at the confirmation of what I am. His two friends remain quiet, taking their orders from him. He's in charge and because of this, I know he's going to be the hardest to take out. They'll protect him at all costs.

There's a vampire hierarchy, and in this particular group, he's king. That's not saying much, as from the looks of their clothes and abilities, they're on the bottom of the totem pole of vampires. The higher up the rungs, the more powerful and better dressed you'll find them. The top of the top are swathed in gaudy jewels and designer wear, showcasing one of their greatest sins—greed. I can see them for the monsters they are, but the top echelon have the ability to cloak themselves to humans.

You'll rarely see a top-rung vampire on the streets. Those spineless swine choose to let the others do their dirty work, while they enjoy the spoils—much like their savior.

I stand to my feet, motioning for them to bring it.

The vampire in charge nods his head, giving the others clearance to attack.

"Aww, isn't that sweet," I mock. "You two need permission. Must suck being the weakest links."

The one closest to me bares his teeth, showcasing his elongated canines. Pretty pathetic compared to others I've seen. Tonight alone, I've gone up against scarier.

I quirk a brow at his pathetic attempt to frighten me.

"Honey, I've seen scarier things roaming Jackson Square in the daytime. You really need to practice your fear factor," I goad, trying to get a rise out of him. The angrier they get, the sloppier they fight. Demons are too proud for their own good. Injure their pride and you're already ahead.

"Bitch," he spits, and I cackle, throwing my head back, and that's when the two goons rush me, but I expected as much. They fight dirty, because otherwise they'd never stand a chance, and they know it.

I wait until they're near enough for me to kick out into what can only be described as the splits, knocking both of their heads back so hard that they each fly backward, giving me time to slam back to the ground, unsheathing the sword at my back.

Not giving them a chance to retreat, I step forward, swinging the blade through the air, and slice the closest vampire's head clean off his shoulders. It drops heavily to the ground, rolling to the feet of his king of the night. He kicks the head away, motioning for the other to attack. There's no love amongst monsters. They simply run in packs in order to wreak havoc on the city they infest.

I roll my eyes. "Have you learned nothing? You're both dying tonight."

His head tips back and he shrieks into the night once more. I shrug at the approaching demon.

"Guess you choose death."

I inhale, concentrating on moving the stored electricity through every synapse. It rushes over me like waves on a shoreline. My body tingles and every hair stands on end as I push the energy out of me and into the sword in my hands.

"*Patet via lux et tenebrae*," I whisper into the night.

Light the way and clear the darkness.

My eyes open in time to see the weaker vampire running toward me. I lift the sword and, without preamble, run it straight through. The demon disintegrates into thin air, allowing me to swing around just in time to lop off the head of the one who was supposed to be the leader.

Pathetic.

Sheathing Solis—my trusty sword—I huff out a frustrated laugh.

"That wasn't even fun."

Slow clapping begins behind me, and I don't need to turn to know Zeke's found me. It's not hard when we both are

17

drawn to the demons' presence. It's like my own personal beacon, and Zeke never fails to follow it.

"Impressive, Tori."

"Very valiant of you to watch without offering help," I say tersely, annoyed at his presence.

"Didn't look like you needed help. I was enjoying the view," he says, looking me up and down. "You look good in leather."

"Good deity. Do those lines really work with the human girls?"

He barks out a laugh. "Always with them, never with you."

"And they never will."

"I like the chase."

"You should stop. You're wasting your time," I say, moving past him. "Why are you here, anyway?"

"We cleared an alley north of here. Five vamps had a girl trapped."

"Is she okay?" I ask, spinning toward Zeke.

"She will be. I compelled her to forget and sent her on her way."

I nod my head, pleased that the girl wasn't hurt.

"Any other sightings?"

"Not tonight. It seems abnormally quiet for this time of year."

He's not wrong. Typically, springtime in New Orleans is crawling with vampires. Add mayhem like Mardi Gras, and the evil descends. I don't know what to make of the change. It has been unusually quiet for months, and nothing good can come from that.

"Where are your human pets?" I jab, truly only caring about one.

I've never met the human hunters, but that doesn't mean I haven't run into them many times. There's a particular redhead that has it bad for Zeke, and based on the way she looks at him, they've been together.

"I fought alone tonight," he says, staring at me a little too intently.

"You took on five vampires alone?"

He shrugs like it's no big deal. I've taken on more, but despite Zeke's insistence that he's the toughest hunter out there, we both know that I am. I fell to Earth as one of the strongest virtue angels. In angel hierarchy, I was several rungs above where Zeke had ever been.

"Good for you," I say, lifting my hand and breaking the veil I'd placed on the alley to keep innocent bystanders from happening across my run-in with the demons.

It's imperative that humans remain in the dark about the evil that walks alongside them in the shadows. Humans aren't capable of handling such news. Widespread hysteria would ensue, giving the demons no reason to hide. They'd revel in the fear and feed on the souls of the damned still living.

It's the only reason I can imagine that God allowed us to carry any of our powers to Earth. We don't have them all, but we do retain the necessities: strength, speed, energy absorption, elemental control, mind control—compulsion—and glamour. Add to that impressive list the innate ability to track down ethereal objects—not ethereal beings—and now I have Solis at my back.

"I'm sorry about earlier, Tori. I shouldn't push you into something you clearly don't want. I'll stop."

Lies. He's said this so many times I've lost count.

"What's the draw, Zeke? I don't get why of all the women on Earth, you keep coming back here. I've done nothing but push you away since the day you saved me. Why would you do that to yourself?" I ask, but I already know the answer.

Because we were good together.

When I gave in to my need for Zeke, it was like two stars crashing together. Two celestial beings with energy coursing through us made for one hell of a climax. I can't imagine he has the same experience with any of his human conquests.

The thought sours my already dire mood, but I smash it down, unwilling to go there.

"Maybe I like a challenge," he drawls lazily, that roguish smirk almost doing me in. I know that as long as I'm on Earth, he won't stop tracking me. Why? Because despite my insistence otherwise, we're drawn to each other. Call it spiritually connected if you want.

We're the only two—from what we've uncovered—who've experienced Heaven and are stuck here on Earth due to our own choices. Zeke claims he doesn't want back in, but I know the truth. He doesn't believe it's possible. If he can't achieve it, he thinks it better to delude himself into believing Earth is the best choice. If he tells himself enough times that this place is great, it just might become great. It won't.

"It's not a challenge; it's a flat-out refusal," I shoot back, hoping he'll take the hint and leave me alone.

I'm tired of this dance we're doing. A part of me wants to give in, but I know it's not in either of our best interests. Why can't he allow me to do the right thing?

"I could never have an honest relationship with anyone else, Tori. Even if I did try to share my past with someone, I couldn't tell them everything. There will always be that divide, and it's not what I want in a relationship."

"We want different things. Where I'm going, a relationship isn't possible."

"When are you going to realize that's impossible?"

He doesn't attempt to hide his loneliness, and it's a feeling I know well. I utilize hunting as a way to pretend I don't need anyone. His vulnerability cracks a layer of ice around my heart, because no matter what, I do care about what happens to Zeke. What he did for me at the beginning I can never repay.

"I know your opinion on the matter, Zeke, but I disagree. It would be unfair for me to tell you otherwise." I puff out my cheeks. "I need you to stop. Maybe we can hunt together," I offer, hoping this gives him motivation to lay off, "but nothing more can happen."

He nods. "Fair enough. I'll take your friendship."

"The innuendos? Will those stop too?" I ask with a quirked brow.

He puts up three fingers in the Boy Scout salute. "On my honor."

"Hmmm." I purse my lips and consider his vow. He seems sincere, and if I'm really honest, I owe him an apology. I've been overly rude just to keep him at arm's length, and all because of my own screwups. Not his. Not that I'll admit that to him.

"Fine. Truce," I say. "But you're buying me dinner."

He laughs. "So, I'm buying my friends now?"

"Who said anything about friends?" I grin wickedly.

"You're a tough nut to crack, Victoria English, but I think I'm wearing you down."

"Buy me a beignet, and you'll be a little closer to the mark."

We walk in companionable silence through the heart of Jackson Square. Vendors line the streets, selling everything from trinkets to card readings. A light fog blankets the ground, while the low glow from the streetlamps casts an eerie haze over the area. I pull my jacket tighter around me, staving off the chill.

"Miss, would you like a reading?" an elderly woman with a hunched back asks from her chair.

"No, thank you," I say, shaking my head.

She stands on wobbly legs, making her way toward me. I keep walking, as that's what you do in Jackson Square. If you make conversation, you'll get talked into buying just about anything.

With my head turned forward, I don't see what jerks me backward. I spin around to the haggard woman staring up at me, mouth agape. How did she make it to me so quickly?

"You're shrouded in darkness," the woman says, voice

shaking. "I-I can't see your light. Who are you?" she murmurs, and I pull out of her grasp.

"You shouldn't touch people," I grate through my teeth. "Never know what you'll stumble across."

Her eyes are wide, scared even.

"Something evil possesses your soul."

"Yeah, well. Tell me something I don't know," I hiss, walking away without another word.

"What the hell was that about?" Zeke asks, lips forming a thin line.

"She's nuts?" I offer, knowing she isn't.

I might not consider myself evil, but according to Heaven, that's exactly what I became the moment I fell. And the evil that possesses my soul? I've been trying to run from it since that very day.

A shiver courses through me, and Zeke pulls me in to his side. My initial reaction is to remain in the comfort of his warm, strong arm, but I resist, shrugging out of his grip. I don't need to send mixed signals.

"What she said," Zeke begins, and I don't stop him. "You're not evil, Tori."

I look up into his sincere eyes that stare back at me intensely. A woman could get lost in those soulful eyes. I've spent so much time trying to push him away. Maybe he's right. Perhaps all my efforts are for nothing, and I'm wasting time on Earth being lonely.

Stop it.

I berate myself internally. This is the very crux of why I keep my distance. When I'm drawn back to memories of the time I fell, I feel out of control. The hurt of betrayal and the emotions that came the moment I landed here on Earth make me rash. I chase whatever emotion will help me forget, and every time, I find myself in Zeke's arms. He's been my crutch, and it's not fair to him.

"I might not be evil, but she's not wrong, Zeke."

"What does that mean?"

I shrug. "My light was destroyed before I ever fell."

MIRACLE

SOMETHING EVIL POSSESSES YOUR SOUL.

It's been three days since Jackson Square and my run-in with the crone. Her words have haunted me to the point that I can't sleep. Knowing that she possibly has more of the answers I seek only manages to make my anxiety worse. I'm exhausted and because of that, I'm unable to produce a storm. My energy is depleted, making it unsafe to hunt. I'm practically useless.

My only saving grace is that Zeke has seen fit to leave me alone. He hasn't come checking on me, and I'm grateful for that. It's given me time to process what the old woman said and to know I want—need—to hear more.

I've never put much stock in the things the mediums in the square say. For one, it's heresy, and for two, most of them are full of shit. They don't truly see the future or read cards. They read people. They tell you what they think you want to hear. It's a scam.

The woman from days ago was not. How much could she possibly know?

I'm about to find out. My feet are moving determinedly toward the spot I last saw the woman. Maybe she has the answers I need to get home, or maybe I'm simply playing with fire. Either way, I've come this far.

Except when I get there, she's nowhere to be found. In her place is a middle-aged woman with wavy raven hair that hangs past her breasts, leaning over a table decked to the nines with all the trinkets that draw in tourists. A fake.

"Care for a reading?" the woman croons. That voice is probably a siren call to the out-of-towners milling about on a typical night in the square, but it does nothing to coax me into her charade.

"The woman that was here the other night—where is she?" I bite out the words, trying to signal I'm in no mood for games.

"It's first come, first serve, and I was here first. I don't know of whom you speak." She flicks her wrist, gesturing for me to go away. I cross my arms over my chest. I'm not going anywhere.

"I'm sensing"—she rubs her chin—"frustration."

I scrunch my nose in distaste. "You can drop the act; I'm not buying it."

She groans. "Then go away so I can make some money."

I take a deliberate step toward her, but she doesn't so much as shrink back. "The woman," I grate. "Where is she?"

Huffing, she sits back in her chair and raises her arms. "You're not buying and I'm not talking."

A growl escapes my lips, but it doesn't change the woman's countenance. She's a scammer through and through. If I don't offer her something, she won't talk. I dig into my pocket and produce a twenty-dollar bill. Holding it between my fingers I say, "Ready to do business?"

She grins and snatches the money out of my hand. "Describe this woman you're looking for."

"Older, hunched back, long grey hair."

She huffs, "Almada. She isn't company you want to keep, girl. She's . . ."

"The real deal?" I deadpan. The woman's lips straighten

into a thin line before she stands and walks around the table so that we're eye to eye.

"Dangerous," she whispers. "Almada's visions aren't something to toy with. Some things aren't for us to know."

My eyes narrow at the sudden concern the woman shows. A moment ago, she was all bravado, but now, she almost seems frightened. "That might be so, but I'll take my chances." I turn to go, but her hand shoots out, grabbing my arm. I turn slowly toward her with one eyebrow raised.

"The things Almada sees can't be undone." She swallows. "People have been hurt."

She *is* frightened. It's there in the moisture she swipes from her brow. In the way her voice trembled when she spoke the words *people have been hurt*. What she doesn't realize is that I'm not human. Some old woman isn't going to hurt me. She can't.

Knowledge can do more damage than any person ever could.

I shake off that thought. "I appreciate your warning, but unless you know where I can find her, we're done here."

"Stupid girl," she hisses, dropping my arm. "She's not here tonight. She'll be on her way to Hebrew Rest."

"The cemetery?"

She nods, taking her seat at the table once more. "Tonight, she cleanses the spirits."

I have so many questions about what that entails, but I'll soon see for myself. "Thank you," I say, leaving the woman behind. But I don't miss the words she hurls at my back.

"Don't thank me for having a hand in your end."

I practically run to Dumaine Street to catch the next streetcar to take me to Hebrew Rest.

The woman's words flitter through my head, making me wonder how bad an idea this might turn out to be, but when I analyze my plan to get back home, the only thing that makes sense is that I need to atone for my sins. I'm convinced that part of my penance here is to turn away from temptation and to fight the evil that plagues these lands. If Almada knows more, I need to hear it. I need to know I'm on the right path.

I never quite make it to Hebrew Rest. Less than two minutes after my butt lands on the seat of the streetcar, I look to my right and there Almada sits. My spine goes straight and my head jerks away from her. It's a feeble attempt to shield myself from her view. There's nobody between us on the near-vacant car.

She's the reason I'm here, but this isn't the place to have the conversation that needs to be had. So I keep my head turned and focus my attention on the torn leather seat at my side. The red fabric is pulling away, allowing the yellow cushion underneath to peek through. It's crazy how mundane things become so fascinating when you're doing your best to ignore the fact that your prayers are about to be answered or shattered into a million pieces. That's the power this heretic holds over me.

I shake the woman from my head, desperate to focus on anything but what's to come. The momentary reprieve is a gift I should not turn my back on. It doesn't last long. The bus grinds to a stop and the driver calls out the location, putting us one block from my stop. I remain focused on the seat.

"Get up, child. We get off here."

Almada.

My head turns to her, eyes narrowed in confusion, but she's already making her way off the streetcar. I scramble to my feet, scampering after her like she's my lifeline. She hasn't stopped, walking ahead with her head held high, sending a message to anyone who passes that she's not to be toyed with. Strength radiates from her. Who is this woman?

When I finally catch up to her, we walk in silence for two blocks, in some bizarre standoff. I'm not sure if it's self-preservation or simply stubbornness; either way, I won't budge first.

"Your control is a testament to your creator, angel," the crone says, and I stop in my tracks.

"H-how do you know so much about me?"

She turns to face me, and I notice that the deep wrinkles lining her eyes and forehead are more pronounced today than they were the other night. It's as though she's aged ten years in a matter of days.

"You're not the only one with secrets, girl," she drawls. "God bestows gifts on many. Even us mere mortals. Only we pay a price for his gifts," she harrumphs. "Seems you don't."

"I've paid the ultimate price," I seethe. "I'm doomed to roam this earth, keeping the lot of you safe. All the while, you, a heretic, get to enjoy your life. You read cards," I spit. "That's not the work of my God."

She tsks. "Who said I read cards?"

"You," I shoot back, becoming frustrated with the detour this conversation has taken. I came for answers about my future, not to talk about what this woman is or isn't.

She shakes her head back and forth. "I wasn't going to be the one to read your cards. I was working in the square with a friend," she explains, sounding defensive. "I don't read cards and I don't accept money for my visions."

My brow raises. "Your visions?"

She nods. "God has given me the gift of sight. I'm a seer."

I huff out a humorless laugh. "God doesn't allow that sort of thing to roam the earth unchecked."

"Yet here you are. A fallen, roaming the earth, seeking me out." She turns on her heels and moves forward in the direction we had been moving.

"I'm only here to figure out how to get back."

"For a celestial being, you are very naïve, child." She doesn't even deign to look at me.

"Stop calling me a child," I bark. "I'm probably older than you are."

She laughs. "True. Yet I age and you don't."

I glance around to ensure we're alone so nobody can overhear the conversation we're having. That's when I realize we're heading in the opposite direction from the cemetery. "Why are we going this way?"

"The dead don't appreciate angels. It's hard to cleanse their souls and send them to the afterlife on a normal night. It'd be damn near impossible to do it with you loitering around," she states, sounding agitated. "Now let's get to why you've sought me out." She pauses once more, facing me.

I take a step toward her, closing the distance to ensure that anyone lurking about can't overhear us. "What you said about my light being shrouded in darkness—"

She shakes her pointer finger back and forth. "That's not what I said. I said I couldn't see your light, and that something evil possesses your soul."

I gulp at the reminder of that less-than-pleasant description. "What does it mean?"

She smacks her lips together. "I think you know very well what it means."

"That because I fell, I'm evil?" I ask, not sure at all.

She frowns. "You can delude yourself as much as you want, but you and I both know that's not the reason evil surrounds you. It's why you fell, Victoria."

My spine straightens and I glare down at the woman. "It's obvious you know a great deal about me, but that's not why I came to find you."

"And now we get to the point," she says. "Go on."

"How do I get back?" I grate through my teeth, trying and failing to be patient with the woman. I feel like she's toying with me. Her arms cross over her chest in what looks like defiance. I take a deep breath and force myself to ask again. Calmly this time. "How do I get back to Heaven?"

She uncrosses her arms and leans in even closer. "You don't."

I blink. All the while, my eyes never waver from the woman. Searching her face, I find no signs of deceitfulness. She believes what she says.

I huff. "Y-you're wrong. There's always a way. Your sight is broken."

"It's not. I see it all clearly, Victoria. Your future is here."

I stagger backward. The world tilts and the sensation of falling sweeps over me. I shake my head, trying to clear out the fog that's settled over me. A pair of surprisingly strong hands grab my shoulders to help stop my swaying.

"Victoria, listen," Almada commands. "There is no way back to Heaven for you. It's not meant to be. When you fell, God made other plans. Heaven hasn't just closed the gates behind you; they've been slammed shut, and all of the repenting you do will never be enough."

My head shakes back and forth violently. This woman can't be right. She has to have her information wrong. God is gracious. God knows what's in my heart. He'd never turn his back on me. Never.

"You're wrong," I spit. Anger claws its way up my spine, and I allow it to burn.

"Know when the fight is over, child, because your time in Heaven has ended. There is much for you to do here."

"Here? Why would I stay here and help a bunch of pathetic humans who sin daily for no other reason but to satisfy their own selfish desires? I won't."

She takes two giant steps back, putting distance between us. "You can run from your destiny, but it will always find you. There is no way out, Victoria. God won't allow it."

"God can't stop me," I yell. "If he won't let me in, then I'll end this miserable life and go on to wherever I'm damned to go."

"Go home," she orders. "Death won't find you."

"Everyone can die." The words are whispered as the fight drains out of me.

"Only if God wills it." She begins walking, leaving me alone on the sidewalk and taking the little hope I had left with her.

REDEMPTION

My feet shuffle through the square, with no real plan of where to go next. People mill about, chatting and enjoying their time, if their laughter is any indication. All I feel is hollow.

Every shred of hope I've held on to was vanquished in an instant. Two words sealed my fate. *You don't.*

My mind screams at me not to believe a word the heretic said, but my heart knows better. The woman wasn't lying. She's seen my future and it's here on Earth. A place I don't want to be. But I don't have a choice. Free will isn't something the fallen are given.

I did this.

A tear drips from my eye, but I don't wipe it away. My feet continue their monotonous pounding of the pavement, with no real direction. My shoulder bumps into someone, but I don't react as they yell, "Hey, watch where you're going!" I'm on autopilot, just barely hanging on by a thread.

Someone walks by, leaning toward my ear. "I know who you are." My head jerks up, but I only see the man's retreating back. Another person bumps into my right shoulder and I turn to see a woman glaring down at me. Her face is distorted as my eyes blink. My vision is going in and out as though I'm looking through a kaleidoscope. "You're not getting out of here," the woman cackles.

"What?" I whisper, dazed and utterly confused by the warped imagery in front of me.

"Wh-who are you?"

The woman throws her head back and cackles louder. My hands fly to shield my ears from the piercing sound, just as someone else runs into my back, shouting for me to move the hell out of their way.

My body begins to shake as I rock back and forth on my heels. My head pivots from one side to the other, watching the crazed woman laughing while a man leers at me. My vision tunnels and I feel the world sway. I'm going down, being pulled under by a current that can't truly exist on solid ground.

Before I hit, a strong pair of arms sweep me up and cradle me into a firm chest. I don't care who this savior is, only that they deemed me worthy of being rescued in this moment. Tears run like a river down my face and into the shirt of that solid chest I cling to. The familiar scent of sandalwood should've tipped me off to the person I cling to.

Zeke.

"Shhh. I've got you, Tori."

Of course it's him. He's always there when I need to be picked up off the ground. It's been that way since day one. My instincts say it's due to the ethereal pull we share, but something deep within questions that theory. I'm too fragile in this moment to examine any other possible reasons.

His strong legs carry us quickly to some unknown location. I don't ask, because I don't care. There isn't a thing in this world I care about. Getting out has been the one sliver of hope I've held on to, and in a matter of moments, that hope's been dashed to shreds.

"Put me down," I whimper.

I'm grateful that he saved me from having an epic meltdown in the middle of Jackson Square for everyone to see, but now, I just want to be left alone.

"No. I'm making sure you're okay." He continues walking at a clipped pace.

"Leave me be, Zeke. I need space."

"No." It's all he says in response, continuing to carry me like a child. His refusal to do the one thing I've asked has that last string of sanity snapping in half.

My fists begin to beat on his chest. "Let me down. Now!"

Zeke finally stops, lowering me to my feet. His firm hands grasp mine, which are balled into fists, holding me still.

"Please calm down. I'm trying to help."

"I don't want your help," I snap. "Can't you see that?"

He takes a deep breath, allowing my hands to drop to my side. "When I stumbled across you in the square, you looked two seconds away from a full-blown panic attack." His hand runs back through his dark hair in frustration. "So forgive me if I misread the situation. I'll leave you to handle things yourself."

He stalks past me, heading God only knows where. He's angry, and I can't say I blame him. For whatever reason, he found me in my moment of weakness. If he hadn't helped me, who knows where I'd be or what would've happened. It was out of pure embarrassment that I pushed him away, and the shame I feel for how I treated him hits me hard in the chest.

"Zeke," I yell to his retreating back. "I'm sorry." My shoulders sag in defeat. All the energy is drained from my body, the fight gone.

With my head lowered, I don't see Zeke stop and head back in my direction.

"You can't keep pushing me away like this, Tori. Friends don't allow friends to break down in public. I only did what I thought you'd want."

My fingers fly to my head, massaging at my temples. A headache is fast approaching.

"Either you want me around or you don't. I won't play the part of your punching bag."

My eyes fly to his. Something akin to panic rises in my belly at the thought of Zeke giving up on me. Despite my actions, he's brought me a sense of security. He's the only other angel I've come across on Earth. He understands me in ways that nobody else ever could, and that's not something I want to live forever without. I reach out to stop Zeke from retreating again.

"Please don't give up on me, Zeke. I-I can't live alone here. I can't be alone."

The tears cascade down my cheeks as the finality of Almada's words settle over me. Zeke's heated expression falls from his face as his arm shoots out, pulling me in to him.

"I don't wanna be alone, Ezekiel. Please don't leave me. Don't stop trying." I can hardly contain the anguish that spills with every word spoken. The mounting fear of being deserted by Heaven and left to this rotting planet tears at my soul.

"I won't ever stop. I can't," Zeke coos into my hair. "Don't you see that? I care too much, Tori."

"They've cast me out for good. I'm stuck here." I cry harder. Every time I consider my new reality, the pain is more intense. Shouldn't the agony ease? Can God not see fit to bestow some kindness on me?

"You were right all along," I say, peering up into Zeke's concerned eyes. "I'm never getting back in."

He swallows hard, lips forming a perfect line. "How do you know this?"

"The woman from the square. I found her."

He shakes his head. "She's a crazy heretic, Tori. Surely you can't believe her."

"Yet I do." My eyelids flutter as I try to remain upright. The lack of energy, coupled with the life-altering news, has taken a toll on my body. I need to power up, but I doubt I could even conjure a slight wind in this shape.

"Whoa. Let's get you home and in bed," Zeke says, lifting me once more into his arms.

Typically, I'd rebel against being carried through the streets of New Orleans like some damsel in distress, but I don't have the energy to fight it.

I don't know how we get back to my loft. Shortly after being hoisted up by Zeke, I dozed off, the last of my vitality zapped from me. When I come to, it's pitch black, save for the thin stream of light floating in through the window. Zeke's heavy breathing is the only sign I'm not alone.

I roll toward Zeke, whose breathing has slowed. The light from the moon illuminates one half of his face, and I can't help but inhale sharply at just how perfect he is. Humans carve stone images in the likeness of men far inferior to this angel. And here I am, curled up next to him. I've been such a fool, treating him like a nuisance.

"You're awake." Zeke's groggy voice filters through the room.

"I am."

He stretches, yawning all the while.

"I'm sorry if I woke you. Go back to sleep." My hand reaches out, moving a stray piece of dark hair out of his eyes.

"You can't sleep?" he asks, eyes fluttering.

I shake my head.

Zeke's hand cups my cheek and I lean into it. "What happened today, Tori?"

I sigh, not sure that I want to get into it, but knowing it's a conversation we're going to have sooner or later. Might as well rip off the Band-Aid.

"She said that God made other plans for me when I fell. Heaven's gates are slammed shut to me." My shoulders lift. "That's basically it."

"You've always believed there's a way. Why now? Why believe a stranger?"

That's the question I don't have an answer to. For whatever reason, I felt the finality in her words. My soul felt the

35

truth in them. How do I explain that to Zeke? He's tried to tell me the same for two years, and I've never once listened.

"If you want back, fight for it, Tori. Everyone is capable of atonement." His eyes bore into mine, willing me to have hope. But all my hope is gone.

"You don't know the things I've done." The words are whispered. "There might still be hope for you. Don't allow me to drag you down."

"I don't care about any of that, Tori. I just want you." He clears his throat. "As my friend," he amends.

"What if it's just our connection to Heaven that has you feeling this way, Zeke? What if it's not real?"

"Does it matter, Tori? Isn't fate designed by Heaven? Do humans question the love they feel for another because it was destined? No. They embrace it, and so should you."

"What if I'm scared?"

"What's there to be scared of? We're on Earth for a reason, and we're lucky to have each other."

I groan, turning my back to him. I don't want Zeke to see my vulnerability. He's already witnessed too much of it tonight. "What if He takes that away from us too?"

"God?"

"Yes. If we're banished to Earth, He doesn't want us to be happy. It's a punishment."

"I'll take whatever I can have of you, for however long I can, Tori." His chest is pressed against my back, and chills race up my spine at the contact. "Whatever it is pulling me to you, it's strong. I don't want to fight it."

A desperate feeling comes over me. A crazed need to be held. To have the events of the night wiped away. I could give in to this intense pull too. I could have more with Zeke. If I'm condemned to this fate, why not allow this? He's as perfect as they come. Looks aside—and those are some impressive looks—he gets me like nobody else ever could. I'm immortal. He's immortal. We could actually have a chance at a future. But he doesn't know my past.

"I'm broken."

"Who isn't?" he counters. "Tori, we both fell. The reasons behind it and the things that have happened since don't matter. They don't define us. They don't define you." He turns me back toward him, putting his fingers beneath my chin and tipping it upward. "All I see when I look at you is a strong, beautiful woman. Nothing evil. Never that."

His words are a balm to my bruised and shattered soul. The way he looks at me, as if he truly sees me, gives me hope I dare not keep. Self-preservation has been my crutch, and losing that now wouldn't be in my best interest. But to hell with playing things safe.

I inhale deeply, relishing the way Zeke makes me feel despite knowing better. I haven't felt like this since—

I pull out of Zeke's grip at the thought of him.

The man who made me fall. The ultimate deceiver.

"Don't do that," Zeke begs. "Don't pull away from me. Don't punish me for the sins of others."

And that's just it. I am punishing him for something he has nothing to do with.

I am broken.

He leans into to my ear and whispers. "I remember a time not long ago when you begged me to touch you, Tori."

I shiver at the reminder of those early days. Days when I was more broken than I am now. More confused and lonely. Those days were my darkest, and I gave into every temptation imaginable, because I felt hopeless. I told myself I was damned to Earth without a chance of redemption. Little did I know I was correct.

"I had you in my arms once, and I know how good that felt. Let go." Zeke lowers his mouth to mine, and I stiffen. "Give in to me, Tori. Let me take care of you."

Some things never change, and in this moment all of my weaknesses are on full display. Without another word, I seal my lips to his. Temptation in the form of man has always been my downfall, and here again I prove that in fact, nothing

37

has changed. I'm already damned. Might as well enjoy the perks.

PLAY WITH FIRE

I woke this morning, wrapped in Zeke's warm embrace, with a new outlook. Earth will be what I make of it, and certainly, having him by my side, it won't be all bad. After our talk, he held me. It was everything I didn't know I needed.

With my new outlook, I managed to drum up a storm. Energy is stored and ready to go, so I can get back to hunting demons. That is normal, and some sense of normalcy is what I need right now.

"What are you smiling about?" Zeke asks from across the table at a small café in the Garden District. We're seated on the patio, enjoying the fresh air.

"I'm excited to hunt."

His eyebrow quirks. "Hunting? That's all?"

"It's been a while." I wink.

"It's been a few days." He chuckles, leaning across the table and taking my hands in his.

"Is there nothing else that excites you?"

"I think you could give me some reasons."

Lifting my hand to his mouth, he places a kiss on my knuckles that's a promise of more to come.

"Would you look at that. Our man Zeke's been keeping

secrets," a gruff man jests as he walks by the café with a group of people.

Zeke's eyes close. "Shit," he says under his breath.

They beeline to the door, and I know it's a matter of time before they join us on the patio.

I remove my hand from his, putting some distance between us. "Who are they?" I ask, not turning to see if they're already behind me.

"People you've made it clear you have no interest in knowing."

Human hunters.

I turn to find four sets of eyes staring me down with varying degrees of interest—and hostility. Three men and one woman. A woman who is definitely plotting my murder in her head, if her deep scowl is any indication. Interesting.

"Guys, this is Tori. She's a . . . friend."

The short, stocky blond man raises an eyebrow. "Friend, eh? Is that what you call it these days?"

The other two guys laugh, while the lone woman continues to throw eye daggers my way.

"What are you up to?" Zeke asks, trying to steer the conversation into different territory, and I'm grateful for it. I don't need these humans, who are already attuned to too much of the celestial world, working out what Zeke and I are.

The blond shifts on his feet, looking to the tall, muscular, brown-haired man to his right, as if to defer to him. This must be the leader of their rat pack.

"We're heading to the north end. A pack of wolves was spotted there last night. We're going to remove them if they're still there," the man explains, standing tall and never once looking in my direction.

I internally huff a laugh at his ridiculous story. Of course I know that wolves equal demons. If he's not exaggerating about it being a pack, that's ambitious for a group of powerless mortals to take on. This human is either extremely brave or entirely too stupid. Which is exactly why I've chosen to stay away. That type of unjustified bravado will get them killed.

"We'd ask you to join us, but, well, it looks like you're otherwise detained."

"Detained?" Zeke chuckles. "I'm in no way being held against my will." Zeke looks at me and winks.

"Leave them to their date," the girl barks. "I want to grab something to eat beforehand."

The leader levels her with a glare. "We probably should go. I don't want the d— err, wolves getting away."

"You can speak freely about demons to Tori. She's a hunter too."

My head snaps to Zeke's, and I laser him with my best *what the fuck* face. He shrugs, which only makes my spine straighten more. Thankfully, we're alone on the patio, save for the human hunters.

"She's a hunter?" the tall redheaded beauty spits out, crossing her arms over her chest. "I doubt that."

"Maeve, knock it off," the blond guy chastises. "Your jealousy is showing."

"I'm not jealous," she lies. "You're drooling enough for the both of us."

Zeke smothers a laugh behind his closed fist, and I glower in his direction.

"My bet's on Maeve throwing down before the night's over," the third guy, who looks an awful lot like Maeve, chimes in. "This one's lethal when she's pissed." He gestures toward the girl.

"I might murder you in your sleep," she threatens, and the rest of their group hoots in laughter.

While the blond and possibly brother-and-sister combo argue about who'd come out on top, I squirm under their leader's intense gaze. I don't know what he's looking for, but he's sizing me up, and based on his narrowed eyes and downturned lips, he finds me lacking.

Good. Let him underestimate me.

41

"Let's join them." The words are out of my mouth before I can even consider what I'm suggesting. Zeke's eyebrows both shoot up in surprise.

"Are you sure? You don't have to do this, Tori."

I stand, straightening my shoulders. "I'll fight with you, but if any of you do anything stupid, it'll be the last time you hunt in New Orleans."

Maeve harrumphs. "You going to take that sass, Danny? We are the hunters around here."

Danny—the blond—hushes her.

The leader steps forward, extending his hand. "I'm Blaine. Zeke's vouching for you and I trust his judgment. He'll vouch for us too. We don't take risks."

There's nothing but sincerity in his words. I've never been for hunting alongside mortals, but I'll make an exception this once.

I shake his hand. "Tori. You help take down these demons and you can call me Tori."

Thirty minutes later, we're walking up to an abandoned house in the north end. The windows are boarded up and the paint is peeling away from the wood. It's hard to know how long this house has been vacant, but by the looks of the entire block, this area has been shut down for years. Not a soul is in sight, which is great news considering a horde of demons lie in wait behind those walls.

"Ready for this, blondie?" Danny jests, and I smirk.

He has no idea just how ready I am. I'm powered up and ready to kick ass.

"Do you plan to use Solis?" Zeke whispers into my ear, and I shake my head.

I'm going to try not to. Solis isn't your typical sword, and it would be hard to hide its power from the group. I have enough pent-up anger and frustration to tear this entire building down. Hopefully, I won't need him tonight.

"Let's do this," I say, motioning for the humans to enter first. Even though the area seems deserted, I don't want to take chances. I place a glamour around the house, shielding us from any passersby. There will be no human casualties tonight.

As soon as I step through the threshold of the dilapidated structure, I feel the evil. It pulses through the room, vibrating the walls and shaking the unsteady floorboards under my shoes. The peeling wallpaper gives way, and that's when I see the blood trickling down the walls and pooling onto the floor.

How many people have been dragged into this place, never again to see the light of day? How many unknowing victims came of their own free will, simply following the lure of sin and sex and false promises whispered in their ear? A literal house of horrors is where these demons have lured us. It has no effect on angelic beings, but the humans aren't protected.

I rush through the foyer and down a dark hallway, following the scent of demonic muck. Rounding a tight corner, I nearly trip over the redheads, who are at the back of their pack. With their ears pressed against the wall, they attempt to make out what lies on the other side. How many are we up against?

It doesn't matter, and the longer we stand here, the more likely we'll give ourselves away. Having the element of surprise on our side gives the humans a better chance of making it out of here alive.

I walk right past them, but Zeke's arm shoots out, stopping me.

"What are you doing?" he hisses. "You can't just bust in there."

"Why?" I whisper, my brow peaked in confusion.

His eyes dart around at the humans, seeming to convey

that we can't use our typical abilities while in their presence. Which only reminds me of why I haven't hunted with them before. I'd momentarily forgotten, but what does that matter anymore?

I have done everything in my power to conceal my celestial heritage, because it's the law, but I've been banished from Heaven. Their law no longer applies to me. If I'm going to be stuck on this Godforsaken Earth, I'm going to embrace exactly what I am.

I lean in close. "Maybe we shouldn't hide anymore."

With that, I kick open the door that separated us from the demons. Quickly scanning the room, I note that there are over a dozen of them crammed into this one section of the house. Who knows how many more are lurking?

"Ah . . . something angelic this way comes," a red-skinned demon sings, sniffing the air afterward. "And she's brought dinner."

The way he slurps his tongue has Maeve gagging.

"Sweetheart, you'll need to push down the revulsion and get your head in the game if you're going to be of use to me," I shout at Maeve.

She growls, glaring at me in response. Good. That was the point of goading her. She needs to be good and pissed.

"Brothers, we have a show to go with our meal." The demon claps and the others laugh and jeer at us.

"You want some? Come get it."

The two beefiest of the demons charge my way and I almost laugh out loud. The bigger they are, the harder—and faster—they fall. With a simple roundhouse kick to the jugular and an elbow to the side of the other's head, they're both on the floor groaning.

"Maeve, dagger," I shout, knowing full well she has a small dagger hidden behind her shirt at her back. It won't disintegrate these assholes like Solis would, but it will kill them nonetheless. My energy is all that's needed, and the dagger will act as a conduit. However, that leaves the need for cleanup afterward.

She purses her lip, wasting time.

"Now," I demand, and finally she complies.

The dagger flies through the air and my hand snaps out, catching it by the hilt. I slam the blade into the heart of the first and then the second, while three more demons rush toward me.

I kick the closest dead demon into the feet of those heading my way and they topple like bowling pins. Maeve's blade slashes through skin and marrow to pierce each of their hearts.

"Are you guys going to help?" I call over my shoulder to the group of hunters, who've stood around watching bug-eyed as I single-handedly took out five demons.

From there, it's a cacophony of fists hitting flesh and blades slicing through the air as the humans join the fray. Demons drop all around us, and within minutes, the place is silent. The smell of rotting evil permeates my nose.

"Ugh," I groan. "This is so damn messy."

"As opposed to?" Blaine asks with a raised brow.

Yet another reason I don't fight with humans. Too many damn questions.

"What do we do with all of these? We can't dump this many bodies in the landfill," Danny states.

"You dump demons in a landfill?" My voice pitches.

"Not usually," Blaine cuts in, but he doesn't offer an explanation or go into detail about how they typically dispose of the bodies.

My guess is that's always been Zeke's job, and he's never really shared what he does with them. It's not likely he can simply say, "No worries, guys. I used my heavenly sword and disintegrated them."

While they all fight about who's going to clean up, I make the decision.

"Everyone out," I yell. "We're burning the place to the ground."

Several sets of eyes turn to me in confusion.

"Won't that draw unnecessary attention?"

"As opposed to?" I throw Blaine's words back in his face. "This entire area is deserted. By the time the fire department arrives, the place will be toast. They'll never uncover any of the demons' remains."

"What about the humans they killed here? Don't their families deserve closure?" Maeve practically spits in anger.

"Have you gone upstairs or downstairs to see what's left of those people?" She doesn't answer, so I decide to fill her in. "You won't find anything to determine who they were, and neither would the police. Demons devour every part."

"They could case the place for fingerprints."

I laugh bitterly. "I understand your need for closure, but sometimes people don't get closure. What's more important for the greater good? Identifying a dozen or so dead people, or keeping the human population in the dark about literal demons roaming among them? You open that Pandora's box, and there will be much more bloodshed on your hands."

Danny's face pales and Maeve's turns a bit green, but nobody argues with me past that.

"Out. I'll take care of this," I order, and they all obey.

We didn't bring gas or anything else that could help to light this sucker on fire, so my power will be necessary. I call upon the wind and draw a storm to me. Within moments, lightning strikes overhead and thunder rolls. I throw my hands into the air and summon the energy down around me. A bolt strikes the house, and I direct the flames to encircle the room filled to the brim with the dead. In a matter of moments, the house is on fire and flames are licking at my legs.

I walk through the door just in time for the house to begin to crumble to the ground.

It's all happening far faster than what's humanly possible.

Damage this great would result from something more in line with an explosion, but that's exactly what my powers created.

How I'm going to explain this to Blaine, who seems too curious for his own good, is beyond me, but right now, that's not my problem. I might be playing with fire, but I won't be the one burned in the end.

BELIEVER

"What was that?" Blaine asks, gesturing to the crumbling house. "That's not possible. You couldn't have survived that."

Just as I thought. Blaine can't leave well enough alone.

"Did you search the place? Do you know what those demons had hiding within those walls?" I raise a brow and when he doesn't answer, I continue. "Didn't think so."

"That storm came out of nowhere," Blaine changes tack, but I stay right with him.

"What? Now I control the weather?" My hands fly up in the air. "It's freaking New Orleans, Blaine. I don't control the erratic weather patterns."

"She's right. Cut her some slack. She just cleaned up a mess you weren't going to." Zeke joins the conversation. Finally. "I, for one, am grateful for it. If not for that lightning strike, we'd have some explaining to do when people stumbled upon a house filled to the brim with corpses. Not all human, I might add."

"Something is off." Blaine hurls the accusation at me. "What you did in there"—he shakes his head—"something's off."

Zeke's in Blaine's face before I can even think about intervening. "Knock this shit off. Whatever you think is going on, it's in your head. You can't handle the fact that she's more skilled than you." Zeke shrugs. "Deal with it. We're going home."

Zeke grabs my hand and leads me away from the group. When we're out of earshot, my head turns toward his. He doesn't look at me. I'm trying to gauge just how pissed off he is. After that overshow of power, he's going to have to do damage control. We can't allow Blaine to go snooping around my business, and I know that's just what he'll do. He's asking too many questions, and after tonight, he won't stop unless Zeke steps in.

Using persuasion is dirty, but in times like these, it's imperative. I put him in this position, and I wouldn't blame him for being angry. We walk the whole way back to my house and not once does he look at me.

I sigh. "I'm sorry, Zeke, but what choice did I have? That place had to be destroyed."

"It's not just the house, Tori. You blatantly kicked that door down and incapacitated five demons before any of them could blink."

"I never wanted to fight with humans."

His head snaps to mine, fury radiating from him. His clenched jaw and narrowed eyes make me want to retreat, but I don't.

"You're the one who insisted," he says through gritted teeth. "I asked if you were sure."

"Well, I wasn't," I yell. "My life was just flipped upside down, and then that human girl practically challenged me."

He groans. "Leave Maeve out of this."

"Now you're defending her?" My hands fly up in a *what the actual fuck* expression. "You know what? You should go," I say, turning away from him and heading inside.

I'm halfway up the stairs when he comes bounding up behind me.

"Stop it, Tori. Don't even think about pulling this bullshit. I won't let you push me away. Not after what just happened."

49

"What happened was me taking care of business, Zeke. What I was born to do," I throw over my shoulder, stepping into my room and plopping down on my bed.

"Never in front of humans. You know better."

"I know nothing," I scream. "I'm damned to this place, and the only thing I can cling to is hunting. Now you want me to give that up to fight with some pathetic humans?" I blow out a harsh breath, preparing to send him packing. I'm wiped out from the hunt, and this conversation isn't going to go well tonight.

"You're going to give us away, Tori. You have to be smarter."

"You know what, you're right. You should run away from this," I snap. "You have no idea what trouble I'll bring you. Do us both a favor, Ezekiel, and forget I exist."

He bends down, grabbing me by both elbows and pulling me to my knees so that we're face to face. His chest heaves as he attempts to control his mounting anger.

"That's never gonna happen, Tori. I don't scare so easily. You of all people should know that once I've got something in my sights, I'll move Heaven and Earth to have it."

"I don't know that," I bite. "How would I? I barely know you."

"Do you believe all of the lies you tell, Tori? For two damn years I've pursued you."

"And I've told you to go away," I shriek, growing more annoyed by the second.

He lowers his mouth to my ear. "Except when you don't. You play games, Victoria, and you know it. As much as you try to pretend it never happened, I see you wanting to fall back on that time we shared. You want this as much as I do."

The truth in those words is frustrating. I try to do right by him, but he won't let me. I allow him in, and he tries to change me. It's a no-win situation for both of us, when neither wants to give in fully.

"You can't do this, Zeke. It's not fair. I've done everything

50

to keep you at arm's length, for your own good. But you never listen." I shove him away from me. "You break down my walls and I give in, only for you to try to change me. This is me. I'm not altering who I am for anyone. Especially not for some ragtag group of humans."

"I don't need your protection, Tori. And I sure as hell never asked you to change. I just want you to be safe," he yells. "I just want you."

The room is shrouded in darkness, save for the sliver of light filtering in through the window. The vulnerability displayed by Zeke has me breathing heavily and my eyes dropping to the floor. This is so unlike him, and it's not fair that he feels this way without knowing everything about me.

Can you really start a relationship based on half-truths and unforgivable circumstances?

"If you knew why I fell, you wouldn't think so damn highly of me," I admit, keeping my gaze lowered to the ground.

Zeke's fingers tip my chin up so that he can look directly into my eyes. "I don't care about your past, Tori. I want your future."

"Don't say things like that," I whisper, our mouths mere inches apart.

Zeke forges on with his declarations. "Eternity's a long time to be alone. I want to know everything about you. I want you by my side every day and in my bed every night."

My breath hitches, the power of his words instigating shivers under his touch and leaving me wordless.

"Let go of whatever's holding you back. Let me make you feel good."

What he offers, I know better than to accept. It'll only bring us both pain in the end. I meant it when I said I was broken. There's a piece of my heart that was stolen, and I never got it back. I never will, because the man who possesses it is the epitome of selfishness. He's the keeper of souls and destroyer of life.

"I'm not whoever hurt you, Tori. I'll take care of you."

His words have me feeling reckless. The need to mean something to someone trumps all the reasons I'd concocted to keep my distance, and without thinking, I act.

I crash my lips to Zeke's, begging entrance to his mouth with my tongue. He opens to me immediately, groaning at the desperate feeling of our tongues colliding. I shimmy out of my leather pants while his hands trail from my hips up my side, raising my shirt along with them. He pulls it over my head, so I'm left in only a black thong and matching lace bra. My hands pull at Zeke's shorts and he helps me by stepping out of them.

I bite my lip as my own hands go to my back, undoing my bra and allowing it to drop to the bed. A tug at my hip drops the thong to the floor. I'm bare to him, and his eyes devour me.

"You're going to kill me," he groans into my neck, as he trails kisses up the curve to below my earlobe. "I've wanted this again for so long."

A part of me is screaming to stop before we go too far, but this feels too good to be anything but right. Maybe I'm weak. Maybe I'm not worthy, but right now, I feel alive for the first time in a long time. His expert hands massage and explore places that nobody but Zeke ever has.

"I can't promise you much, but I can give you this."

His brow arches. "What are you offering, Tori?"

"Physical only. Nothing emotional. No titles. No promises." I search his eyes, waiting for his acceptance of my terms. "Can you accept that?"

"It's not what I want."

"It's all I can offer."

He inhales deeply, eyes closing on the exhale. When he opens them again, I see his resolve. He may not like it, but he's not turning me away. "For now."

I lean forward. "Love me," I whisper into his ear, taking his lobe between my teeth and biting lightly.

He pulls back just a bit, looking into my eyes. "Are you sure?"

"Yes," I say, lying back and pulling him with me.

I've only been with him, and it started as one night born from a sheer need to erase the memory of someone else. This time will be nothing like that time.

Whereas the memory brings shame, I want to remember this time as though it were my first. I want Zeke to wipe away my past with his touch alone. No thoughts of another.

"Where are you, Tori?"

"Huh?" I say, my eyes meeting his.

"Your mind was somewhere else. If we're going to do this, I want you here. With me."

That vulnerability is back, despite the alpha in his tone. I lean up and place a kiss on his lips, trying my best to reassure him.

"I'm here. With you."

His eyes look back and forth between mine, and he must find what he's looking for, because he finally relaxes, closing that gap between our bodies. In one smooth thrust he cements our new arrangement.

Sex is one thing I can't fuck up.

RIPTIDE

My legs shake as my fists clench. To say I'm nervous is a gross understatement. I'm petrified. You don't break the laws of God and go unpunished.

I've been summoned to a hearing, and there's no doubt as to why. I gave my angelic name to a human, and every time he calls it out, I go willingly. I'm only to go to Earth on God's command, not at the request of mortals. Yet I have done just that.

Our names are sacred, as we're bound to answer the call. It's the way we communicate in Heaven. Visualize and call out. It's that simple. Now, a human knows my face and has my name. What's worse is that I relish every moment with him. I pray every day that he'll call to me.

Thunder rumbles and I know that God is furious.

In a blink, the council appears, surrounding me on all sides. Their disapproval radiates through me, but it's my brother Michael's condemnation that shames me most. My head bows as I fall to my knees before him.

I listen as he calls out my transgressions one by one. Hearing all the ways I've betrayed God and my fellow angels is worse than I could've imagined. It's painful.

Yet I don't regret a single one of them.

"And therein lies the greatest betrayal of all, Victoria," Michael chastises, reading my thoughts. "You've fallen for a human."

My head snaps up, shaking back and forth violently.

"No. I don't . . . I can't . . . it's not like that."

"Did you or did you not interfere with fate and give your name?" Michael asks in a booming baritone that shakes the cloud I stand upon.

"Under duress, Michael. He caught me off guard." My words spill out in a jumble of pathetic excuses that no angel would buy, let alone Michael, God's right hand.

My words fall short, which is evident by the always stoic archangel's frown. Michael isn't one to show any sort of emotion, and his clear disappointment stings.

I'm dismissed for deliberation, and one hour later the verdict is handed down.

Guilty.

A guilty verdict would typically result in damnation based on my infractions, but Michael and the council see fit to spare me. My punishment is devastating, but more lenient than I deserve. My rapier is confiscated, and I'm banned from Earth.

The latter is the most heartbreaking.

I'm trying to convince myself that life without seeing *him* isn't as bleak as a lifetime in Hell. I'm only fooling myself. Michael was right. I love him.

Victoria.

My name on his lips curls around me like a cocoon. Goose bumps and butterflies race through me as he calls out to me. Every ounce of my being begs to go to him. To be with him. Yet a small voice, not my own, whispers of all the things I'd be giving up. There's a chance he doesn't feel as strongly for me as I do him. Am I willing to fall for a hope and a prayer?

I no more than think the thought before the clouds begin to quake and thunder crashes. God knows my thoughts, and he's sending a clear message. Think carefully, because there is no way back.

55

Victoria.

He calls my name again with a sense of urgency.

I need you. I . . . love you.

My breath hitches and eyes close as I savor the words. How could he have known that's all I needed to hear? Without another thought, I fall.

I jerk awake, panting at the memory turned dream. I haven't thought about that night in years, and for damn good reason. It was the beginning of the end.

I turn on my side to find the bed's empty. Zeke's already left, without saying goodbye. Panic crawls up my chest. Was I talking in my sleep? Does he know my secret?

My hand runs through my hair, pulling at the roots in frustration. Worry and anger war to pull me under—worry over why Zeke isn't here and anger for the intrusion by my past into my dreams. How dare he haunt me. Is it not enough that he ruined my life? Why, the very night I decide to give in to my need for Zeke, would my mind conjure this memory? It's because of him I hardly sleep as it is. It makes me sick that after everything he did, my mind still craves his touch. He left an ache so acute it threatens to tear me apart, no matter how hard I try to reject it. And I hate myself because of it.

Staring at the ceiling, I will my breathing to slow. Getting worked up about something from the past isn't the way to start the day. I refuse to allow him to have this much control over me.

The wooden beams overhead help to refocus my thoughts. They remind me of Zeke. It was he who transformed this hayloft into a livable home. From the polished exposed beams to the treated wood floors, this place has Zeke's touch in every corner. So much thought and hard work went into transforming this space—for me.

The very bed I sleep on was handcrafted by the power angel, soon after I took ownership of the barn and surrounding property. It was Zeke who helped me arrange it all. Without him, I would've been lost in so many ways. He saved me.

That's the difference between the two men. One used me at every turn for his own benefit. He took everything I offered. Zeke has only ever given of himself.

Throwing off the covers, I jump from bed, quickly dressing in my workout gear. First I need to work off some steam, and then I need to find Zeke. Today I'll be training extra hard, just to attempt to wipe all thoughts of that dream away.

Thoughts of him away.

He who shall not be named was my downfall. He's the entire reason I fell, and I'll regret it for eternity. The worst part of it all? It was my decision; he never asked me to. I did that all on my own, and no matter how much time has passed, that truth never gets easier. Placing the blame solely on him does.

Lust is an evil bitch that'll turn on you in an instant, leaving scars that may not be visible but last a lifetime, the pain never dulling.

I chug a bottled water and rip open a protein bar. Angel or no, hunger is still a thing, and this morning, I'm starving. I shove half the bar into my mouth and chew, trying to think of everything I want to accomplish today.

Trying to keep my mind from wandering to people and times I'd best not think about. Things that only stress me out and make me angry. I throw the remaining food in the trash can, no longer hungry, and go through my morning routine. It's accomplished in record time, as the need to get out this loft is suffocating.

Clad in my black sports bra, black shorts, and black Nikes —basically my signature pissed-off look—I head toward the trail behind my loft. Popping in my earbuds, I turn the volume on high, desperate to drown out the residual noise caused by my dream.

I'm not moving as fast as I'd hoped. My powers are weakened from last night, which just manages to piss me off more. I'll need to recharge before tonight if I want to rid the world of more demons. And I do. It's my only mission in this new life.

I let the anger propel me forward on the dirt trail I've run for years. My arms pump and sweat beads on my forehead. It's been unseasonably warm, but I won't let it stop me from pushing myself. I need the burn. Anything to get my mind as far away from him as possible.

I make it a mile before my foot catches on an exposed root, nearly sending me to my knees. I stop in the middle of the path, arms coming up atop my head, bent over, breathing heavily, as treacherous tears stream down my face. All the pain and frustration comes to a head. I don't want to think about the past, yet I can't escape it. I throw my head back and scream, a guttural cry toward Heaven.

The sky opens up and rains down heavy droplets of water, soaking me through. Thunder shakes the earth, and I can't help but feel it's God's way of punishing me for a dream I had no control over.

"What do you want from me?" I yell to whoever is listening, but there is nobody. There hasn't been for some time. They all turned their backs the day I decided to trade in my wings for a chance at love.

My heaving breath is so loud that I almost miss the cracking of branches behind me. I still, wiping away the lingering tears, focusing my ethereal hearing on whatever or whoever is approaching.

The hairs on the back of my neck stand on end. Something's off. It's the middle of the day, and even with the overcast it's far too light for what I'm sensing. Whatever is approaching isn't human and it isn't exactly animal. It's pure evil.

Another branch cracks right behind me.

I swing around, fists at the ready, but they're caught midair by a wide-eyed Zeke.

"Calm down, killer." He chuckles but stops short when he sees something on my face.

Fear.

"What's wrong?" he asks, swiveling his head to take in the area.

My shoulders relax slightly, breathing coming under control as I process it was just Zeke.

"You scared me. I thought—"

"That someone was sneaking up on you?" he says, cutting me off.

"Yeah, I guess," I kick at the dirt, sending pebbles racing across the ground, feeling foolish.

"You looked like you were having a moment," he admits, brows creased in the center, worry evident in the way his lips pinch at the corners. "This isn't about last night, right?"

My cheeks heat at the knowledge that he witnessed such a personal meltdown and at the memory of what we did. I blow out a breath. "No. Of course not. I—" I pause, searching his face for hints as to what he might know. There's nothing there. He looks worried, but not angry. "Why did you leave this morning without waking me?"

"I wanted to get in a quick workout," he says, motioning toward his running gear. "Did you miss me?" He grins, pulling me toward him.

"I'm all sweaty," I protest, but it doesn't stop him from bathing my neck in kisses. "Maybe we should go back inside?" I moan.

He steps back, smirking. "Nope. Let's finish this run. You need your strength." He winks before taking off past me, kicking up dirt in his wake.

I sprint after him, and when I finally catch up, we run side by side in silence, each pushing the other to run harder. It's great motivation having a warrior angel train with you. It's also a personal penance. Watching his muscles flex is torture, which only spurs me to pump my arms faster. The lure to join Zeke back in my bed is overwhelming.

Despite having Zeke here, I still can't quite shake my unease. Something niggles at the back of my conscience. The hairs on my neck are still upright, and that makes no sense. I have acute demon radar and it's never off, but it's daylight and impossible. They've never wandered this far out of the city either. Too many signs point to a misfire on my sensor.

Still, I have an intense feeling I'm being watched. Someone other than Zeke is here.

"Did someone follow you?" I ask, turning my head toward Zeke.

He frowns. "No. I'm alone." He slows to a stop, turning toward me. "What's this about, Tori?"

"Someone's here. I can feel them."

WOLVES

He turns in circles, crouching into a fighting stance. He doesn't question my instincts, and I file that away, remembering to buy him dinner sometime. The fact he has my back so readily warms me, endearing him to me even further.

More cracking sounds reach us. With each snap, whatever's out there moves closer. I join Zeke in a crouched stance. From out of the thick brush, two demons step onto the path, heads tilted, sniffing the air with bloodlust. The taller of the two is missing his nose, nothing but two holes in its place. His eyes have no pupils; white nothingness stares directly at me. The skin around his eyes hangs loose, the muscle below exposed. Long, greasy black hair falls to his shoulders. He looks like he just came from a fight and he lost.

The other has the head of a wolf, yellow eyes large and dilated. He stands on two feet, swaying back and forth.

What the hell?

"Are you seeing this?" I call over my shoulder to Zeke, not willing to risk turning my back on the monsters.

"I've gotta say, I'm not feeling good about this turn of events," Zeke admits.

He can say that again. It's been years since I've come against anything other than a vampire, and it's been a millennium since I've encountered a werewolf. Worse yet, they're out during the day. That is something I've never witnessed. Demons are typically eviscerated by the sun, which makes it impossible for them to roam during the day.

It was one of the curses God put on Lucifer when he was banished to Hell. Eternal darkness for him and all the original fallen angels. This new development is bad. Very bad.

My eyes roam the two creatures, looking for anything that would help me understand how they're out.

"One of you wanna tell me how you're still standing? Considering the sun is out," I say, lifting my chin upward.

No-nose steps forward. "Things are changing," he says. His voice slithers over me, menacing and malicious. "The days of hiding are almost over."

My eyebrow rises to a point. "How?" I spit the word.

The wolf throws his head back and howls, while the other laughs maniacally.

"Friends." It's all he offers.

Witches.

The only thing that makes sense is that the witches have teamed up with Lucifer, but what's in it for them? The covens around here don't play nice with any creature. They keep to themselves and don't get mixed up in the celestial politics that the rest of us are forced to partake in.

The werewolf raises a fur-thick paw to scratch at his ear, and that's when I see it—the talisman on his finger. Definitely witches.

There are different covens all over Earth, and each sides with either Heaven or Hell. One faction wants peace and to be left to themselves, while the other wants hell on Earth and to reign supreme. Dark witches are at work here.

"You stumbled across the wrong fallen today, boys," I say, lacing as much conviction as I can muster into my threat.

"We're going to feast on your heart, angel." He growls the word like a curse.

As much as I want to unleash my signature brand of

cocky, they've caught me off guard. I have the benefit of Zeke's help, but we're unarmed. Neither of us has our swords on us, and unless Zeke has powered up, we're at a major disadvantage. This fight isn't going to be one of the easiest I've embarked on. I grit my teeth.

"Smell that, Magrid?" No-nose directs to the wolf. "Fear. She's going to taste delicious."

I huff. That's good. Underestimate me. That'll work well for you, I think to myself, channeling all the rage I can muster up. It comes much easier than anticipated, the lingering anger from my dream sweeping over me.

No-nose slinks toward me, his left leg dragging behind him at an odd angle. He definitely lost a fight recently. Or he was tortured.

I glance in Zeke's direction, and he smirks, noticing what I had already worked out.

Homeboy making his way toward me is going to be easy peasy to take out. It's the wolf I have my eye trained on.

Zeke steps in front of me, seemingly eager to take out No-nose. "Mind if I take this one?"

"Help yourself, but don't think I don't notice you're taking easy street."

He grins, right before crouching and jumping up into a roundhouse kick, knocking No-nose back a good ten yards. When he lands on his feet, he looks back at me, chest all pumped up as though he has something to brag about. Yeah, so what if he didn't even break a sweat.

"I've seen more impressive takedowns." I shrug, biting my lip in a playful manner.

The truth was, watching Zeke work is sexy as hell. That I can admit.

He laughs. "You like me, English. It's written all over your face."

I chuckle, shaking my head. "Don't get cocky. You still have another one to take out, and he doesn't look as easy," I say, nodding my head in the wolf's direction.

"Come get it," Zeke calls out to the wolf, but it doesn't move.

The demon called Magrid throws his head back once more and howls, long and then in clipped yelps. I frown, taking in the peculiar scene, and then it hits me. He's summoning something.

"Zeke, get back. He's calling more."

Zeke frowns as he digests what I yelled. Before he can make sense of it, four more wolves come out of the woods to stand behind Magrid.

"Fuck. Tori, run!" Zeke bellows, backing up quickly to put as much distance as he can between him and the pack. "Tori, I said go," he commands, but I don't move. I won't desert him. He said he wanted to fight alongside me; now's his chance.

"Go," he screams, turning and running toward me.

Seeing his retreat, I decide to heed his words, and I take off as soon as he's past me. I'm running at inhuman speeds, but it's not fast enough. My diminished power is making me damn near mortal. A quick peek over my shoulder proves what I feared—the pack is gaining on us. Zeke is fifty yards ahead of me, faster than I am, but not even he will be able to outrun these demons.

The sky darkens overhead, clouds snuffing out the sun. Within seconds, the area is shrouded in darkness. They're controlling the elements. Not. Good.

I look back again, and the yellow eyes glowing in the dim light have me pumping my arms faster. My mind walks through all my options at warp speed. Without Solis, my chances of taking all five of the wolves is bleak, even with Zeke's help. We're in uncharted territory. I have no idea of the strength these creatures possess. My run-ins over the past several years have been exclusively with vampires.

That's when all hope is lost. Ahead of Zeke, another pack of werewolves step into our path, surrounding us at our front and back. Zeke and I put our backs together, each facing one of the packs.

"What do we do?" I ask, trying to keep my voice steady, not willing to show fear.

"Go for the pack leader's heart. It's all I've got, Tori. It has to work," he says, squeezing my hand.

"Can using their name benefit us?"

"I'm not sure. Call it out and see," he suggests.

"Magrid, freeze," I yell out, shaking my head at the lameness of my command.

A loud roar shakes the trees and ground beneath us. My eyes widen, not knowing what the hell's happening. Did his name cause this reaction?

Even the wolves stop in their tracks, sniffing the air and looking around. Whatever's out there has even the demons shaken. Magrid's jowls open into an intimidating smile, and I know that using his name doesn't have the same effect as calling out an angel's.

"Shit," I curse, beginning to lose my cool. "It didn't work."

"Tori, listen to me," Zeke whispers. "When I say go, run to your left into the trees. Our best chance is to lose them while most of them are distracted."

I nod my head, unable to speak.

The loud roaring continues, and I cover my ears with my hands, trying to drown out the unnerving sound.

"Go," Zeke says, and I take off, running through the overgrown forest. Branches scratch at my exposed skin, tearing flesh wounds that will heal much slower than usual, considering my powers are drained.

The bushes on both sides of me rustle, signaling I'm not alone. The wolves are closing in, and I'm not sure how many followed me. The only thing for me to do is face the threat head on, no matter the cost. I'll never outrun them.

I stop, turning to assess the situation.

All of them followed me.

There are two angels in these woods, but they all decided to follow me and leave Zeke.

That doesn't add up. I might be stronger, but these creatures wouldn't be able to determine what my powers are. They aren't strong enough. These are bottom feeders.

The pack moves slowly toward me, tongues hanging out and clawed paws hanging to their sides. One's missing. The original wolf, Magrid. My head turns left and right looking for the leader. My heart rate accelerates as I realize what a mess I've found myself in. I never leave my loft without at least one blade.

I was distracted. Again.

Sweat trickles down my cheek from the exertion of trying to escape. I wipe it away roughly, unwilling to go down without a fight. I crouch low in a fighting stance, hoping to take them out at their feet.

The roaring starts up again, but I don't pay it any attention, my focus on the pack. The sounds of heavy feet can be heard breaking branches under their weight. I squint, trying to see what's headed my way. The current head of the pack seems to decide to bring his attention back to me.

He licks his lips, showcasing a row of razor-sharp teeth. I inhale deeply, trying to remain focused as he stalks toward me. He doesn't make it far before a massive dog appears through the trees, baring his teeth.

Hellhound.

My eyes go wide at the sight of the beast. Lucifer's personal pet. If that thing is here, Lucifer's close by. An alarming shiver runs down my spine. They don't leave Hell without him.

In a strange turn of events, the beast rips through the pack, tearing them limb from limb. Sinew and entrails spray everywhere, the forest floor painted in blood, and I'm rooted in place, unable to move. This is my chance to escape, yet I can't get my feet and my head on the same page. You can't outrun a hound.

Hellhounds have one master. They don't care if you're on Lucifer's side or not. They'll rip through you to get to their target, as witnessed here.

When every last one of the demons is torn apart, the hound turns toward me. It moves slowly in my direction, crouching low and revealing its yellowed teeth, pieces of flesh stuck between the blades.

My stomach rolls and I'm close to spilling its contents on the forest floor. The only way to kill a hellhound is with my divine blade, which is currently MIA. The beast takes off in a sprint, coming right toward me. It prepares to pounce and my eyes close as I fall to my knees.

The expected impact never comes. Body shaking and breath heavy, I open my eyes and twist to see the hound chewing what's left of the wolf, Magrid, that had been missing from the pack. The hellhound leapt over me to take out a demon?

Hellhounds are the most vicious creatures of Hell. They don't discriminate when it comes to their victims. Evil, angelic, human—they're all fair game when the beasts are hungry, and they're always ravenous. But why had it passed me by to get to the demon?

I stand slowly to my feet, the hound's eyes never leaving me as it continues to feast on the fallen demon. Carefully, trying to draw little attention to myself, I back up, trying to retreat while the thing's preoccupied with feeding.

I haven't gotten far before it's done, swiping its massive tongue out to wipe the gore from its jowls. I freeze, not wanting to force the creature to attack prematurely. The hound freezes, ears perking up. I strain to attempt to hear whatever has its attention, but I hear nothing. Whatever calls to the beast is for its ears only. It turns away and runs off into the forest without giving me a second glance.

SOMETHING JUST LIKE THIS

I stare in shock. Hellhounds don't leave behind survivors. Their bloodlust is unquenchable, never satiated.

"Tori," Zeke yells out minutes later, sounding frantic.

"I'm over here," I call back, still in disbelief and unable to move from the spot I'm currently rooted to.

He comes barreling through the overgrowth, pulling me into his hard chest, squeezing a bit tighter than is comfortable. My entire body shakes in his embrace, the aftereffects of the adrenaline still attempting to find an exit.

"Are you okay?" he asks into my hair, placing a kiss on top.

I nod, wondering how he's in one piece. There was a herd of demons chasing after him.

"How did you escape?"

"I got far enough ahead and scaled a tree. They were bottom feeders," he explains. "Too stupid to track me correctly."

I let out the breath I've been holding, glad that we're both okay. That was an ambush, and neither of us were armed or powered up.

After several minutes of standing here, me still in Zeke's arms, he steps back, putting space between us, looking me over head to toe.

"Was that a hellhound?"

I nod again.

"How are you still alive?" he asks, with a hint of awe.

"Your guess is as good as mine," I reply, walking back toward the path, wanting desperately to get out of these woods.

"What do you think's happening?" he asks from behind, and I don't bother turning around.

"I don't know. I'm clueless."

"Are you okay?" he asks, but I don't answer. The need to get back to my loft and to some sense of safety is my only goal at the moment. "Stop, Tori." Zeke's demanding tone leaves no room for argument.

I slowly pivot to face him. His eyes are weary as they rush over me.

"What do you expect me to say? No, I'm not all right," I admit, throwing my hands in the air. "Demons in the daytime, werewolves, hellhounds—nothing is all right with any of that," I screech, pressing the palms of my hands into my head and kneading roughly, trying to stave off a headache. When my arms drop to my sides, the world starts to tilt until it's in a full spin. My vision goes blurry and the last thing I see, before everything goes black, is Zeke's concerned face.

When I come to, I'm lying in my bed back at the loft. I stretch my arms over my head, relishing the pull of my muscles. How I got back here is answered quickly, as a half-dressed Zeke leans over the bed, handing me a glass of water.

"Did you lose your shirt?" I prod, smirking, hoping to divert attention from my blackout.

He grins back. "It was dirty. I thought it was more important to make sure you were okay." He looks at me, appearing contemplative. "Wanna tell me what happened back there?"

I groan. "This again? I told you I have no clue."

His brow rises. "I mean why you fainted."

"Oh. That," I say pensively.

"Yeah. That." He frowns. "Not what I've come to expect from the ever brave and tough-as-hell Victoria English."

"Ha. That was a damn ambush."

"I've never encountered anything like that. What do you make of those demons?"

I sit up, taking a long drink of the offered water and placing it on the nightstand when I'm finished.

"My best guess is a coup, and witches are at the helm."

"You think they're after us?"

"Who else? There's nobody else here." I throw my hands out, motioning around.

"But why witches?"

"I don't think they have anything to do with the attack, but they're clearly responsible for the demons' ability to walk in the daylight. The wolves were wearing talismans."

He nods, inhaling deeply. "What's their angle?"

I shrug. "Your guess is as good as mine. Maybe they want my sword in exchange for helping the wolves get rid of us?"

"That makes sense, but Michael won't allow that. Angels will be all over the place soon," he says, looking at me a little too intently.

"Why the hell would Michael care? We're fallen. They have no reason to save us."

"They might not care about us, Tori, but they won't want an ethereal object in the hands of black witches. They also won't stand around and allow demons to walk in the daylight. That would be the beginning of the end."

I huff, "I don't want to see any of those jackasses."

Zeke chokes out a laugh. "Those asses were once your brothers."

"They had no problem watching me fall. They're no brothers of mine."

His mouth forms a tight line. "I'll be right by your side. I won't let them touch you, Tori."

"Who? The angels or the demons? Since apparently they're all coming for me."

"Both," he stresses. "But the angels aren't coming here for you."

"No shit. We both know they've slammed their gate on me."

"That's in the past. It's you and me now."

I let Zeke's words fall over me, cocooning me with his promise of protection. I'll never understand why he's so hellbent on defending me, but I'm not going to look a gift horse in the mouth.

"Tori . . . I want to talk to you about something, but you're not gonna like it." My arms cross over my chest, already geared up for another fight. Zeke groans. "Just hear me out before you go getting moody."

My hand flutters in the air, signaling for him to proceed.

"With the arrival of the new demons and their working with the witches, we're going to need all the help we can get."

"What are you proposing?"

"Blaine and his group."

"No."

"Tori, see reason." Zeke grunts. "They are good hunters."

"They're weak and slow. Things have progressed beyond their capabilities. It'll only get them killed."

"Can't you feel it, Tori? Something has shifted. They can join the fight, and die helping the cause, or they can be sitting ducks with the rest of the human population and die anyway. At least in my scenario, they leave this earth as heroes in their own right."

His hand darts out, moving a piece of my long blond hair behind my ears. I nuzzle into his palm, needing the comfort that Zeke offers in that simple touch.

"What will Michael and his minions think about that?" I purse my lips.

"I don't give two fucks, T. They abandoned us here to make do in our new circumstances. If we join forces with a group of mortals to rid the world of demons, what are they going to do about it?"

"End us and your human friends?"

"Then I guess you get to leave Earth sooner than you thought."

I scoot to the end of the bed, coming to sit up on my knees. Running my hand down Zeke's arm, I lean in and say, "I was just starting to like my circumstances."

His lip quirks into a sexy-as-sin smirk. "Is that so?"

I nod my head, smiling flirtatiously up into Zeke's big blue eyes that match the color of my own. "In fact, I think we could find something to do to tip the scales even more in Earth's favor."

His brow quirks. "Do tell."

I place a kiss on his lips, lean into his right ear, and whisper some salacious ideas. Zeke doesn't waste another second, lowering me to the bed and trailing his kisses south. Right where I want him.

An hour later, we're dressing and heading downstairs to set up a makeshift training facility. If we're going to get Blaine's crew involved, we need to determine just what they're capable of. They know about demons and it's time they learn that there are other supernatural beings roaming Earth. Only then can they have any hope of being useful in the coming fight. That's a conversation for another day. Getting prepared is the current goal.

"I'm starving," Zeke says, after what's likely been four hours of back-breaking labor, trying to get this place in shape. "Wanna go grab dinner?"

"Not exactly. Why don't we do a night in?" I waggle my brows suggestively.

"What, pray tell, do you have in mind?"

I saunter toward him, swaying my hips suggestively, hoping to send the signal that all I want is him. All of him. My hands go to his shoulder and I lean up on my tiptoes, pressing my mouth against his. He moans into my lips, grabbing me by the hips and pulling me flush against him.

"You're playing a dangerous game. We may never eat."

I chuckle. "I'd be okay with that."

"Me too." He places a chaste kiss on my lips and looks down at me. "I wanted to take you somewhere nice. On a date."

"Zeke," I warn. "Physical only. I told you no relationships, and dates equal more. I just want this."

"It's just food, Tori. It doesn't have to be anything more."

He says the words, but the tone of his voice and the way his jaw is working give him away. He's angling for more, no matter what our agreement was. I should've known he'd never truly settle.

"You don't mean that. You never intended to stop pushing, did you?"

"Friends eat together, Tori. Stop making it more than it is."

I sigh. "Food? Yes. Dinner date? No. Okay?"

He hugs me before stepping back. "Pizza work?"

"Pizza would be perfect." I smile. "You go to town and grab that, while I shower and pick out a movie."

"Who said anything about a movie?" He guffaws, trying and failing to muster the appearance of being alarmed by the thought.

"It's just a movie, Zeke. Friends watch movies."

He smirks. "Whatever you say, English."

I want to push my assurance that watching a movie is innocent, but instead, I drop the conversation for now.

"Nothing too girly, please."

"Don't worry, big guy. I won't pick some sappy romance." I roll my eyes.

"No dramas either. Comedy or Marvel. We could use a chill night for a change."

"Noted."

"Don't plan on hunting either."

My face falls. I thought for sure after dinner and the movie, he'd be up for the hunt.

He steps back into me, holding me close and placing a kiss on my forehead. "Until we know what's going on, we need to be careful. We need to train."

I nod, knowing it's the best strategy.

"Go shower. When I get back, it's just you and me. All night."

"I like the sound of that."

He grins, jogging backward to the truck.

I push away the thought of what havoc demons can wreak tonight and head to shower. I've given my whole life to the cause. Tonight, I'm going to experience a night of human normalcy, in the arms of Zeke—my own alpha hero. Only as friends. Just friends.

Keep telling yourself that, Tori.

STAY

Demons soak into the earth, being dragged back to Hell, where they belong. A few tombstones are overturned, the aftermath of yet another run-in with evil.

Except this time, it wasn't a sanctioned fight, and that truth alone could put me in front of the Divine Council for crimes against God. I managed to escape that fate once, but I'm pushing my luck.

"You came," a masculine voice speaks from between two mausoleums. As he steps out under the moonlight, his face is illuminated, and my breath catches at the sight. He's more handsome than I remembered, standing here in a simple pair of gym shorts and a black T-shirt. He's tall and lean, a work of art.

"What are you doing in a cemetery at night?"

"I am visiting an old friend," he explains, stepping closer to me. "It's peaceful at night. Nobody around to distract me."

I sit, trying to regain my strength. Battling six demons took a lot out of me. I typically have my brothers at my back, but tonight, I came alone. Because he called out for me.

"Why did you call for me?" I ask, looking out the corner of my eye at him.

He takes a seat next to me, spreading his muscular legs out in front of him and leaning back on his elbows.

"I found myself in need of help," he said, sucking in his cheek, giving away the lie.

I raise my eyebrows in challenge, and he grins.

"Okay, so it's a little more than that," he admits, and I can't keep the smile off my face.

"Well?" I press, wanting him to say what's on his mind, hoping there's more to it than him simply needing help but knowing how wrong it is that I hope for such things.

"I can't stop thinking about you, Victoria," he says, turning toward me. "I'm going crazy."

My eyes close, savoring the way I feel at his admission. Too good. Too happy.

Foolish.

I let out a breath and open my eyes. "This is crazy. I don't even know your name. Yet I come running when you call out mine. This is dangerous. You know that, right?"

He grabs my hand, placing it in his lap, and the strangest sensation washes over me. My stomach is in a freefall, chills racing across my skin.

"Luke," he says, so softly I almost miss it.

"What?" My head snaps to him.

"Call me Luke." He smiles coyly, as though it's not something he shares with a lot of people.

I know that's not the case. Humans throw their names around like it's no big deal, because on Earth, it isn't. Perhaps Luke's current manner is a result of remorse, because he recognizes the position he's put me in. My name is sacred, and anyone other than celestial beings having possession of it is forbidden.

That ship's sailed. He does know my name and he did use it. Even if that's wrong, I don't want to think about it while I'm here with him. He's shared something with me, and I'm going to cherish that for the rest of my existence, because nobody has ever shared anything with me.

"Luke," I say, testing the name out and loving the way it rolls off my tongue.

The quiet of the cemetery washes over us, but it's not unnerving in the least. Crickets chirp and the leaves on the trees rustle, creating a soothing melody that calms me for the first time in centuries. I could stay here forever with Luke at my side, and that reality is what finally has me snapping out of the fantasy I've allowed to play out for far too long.

"I have to go," I say, attempting to stand, but Luke pulls me down.

I trip and land on top of him. He rolls me so that I'm under him, breathing heavily and looking up into his deep green eyes, wanting things I shouldn't for the first time in my entire existence, with a human I've met only twice.

His eyes roam my face, and I squirm under his intense scrutiny.

"You're beautiful," he whispers, cupping my cheek in his hand. I lean into his touch, basking in his compliment, never wanting this moment to end. "You've bewitched me, Victoria. I don't know how to move on from this feeling."

I turn away from his passionate gaze, cheeks heating. I'm probably caked in demon blood, and that thought makes me self-conscious, a sentiment entirely foreign to me. My hand runs back through my hair, trying desperately to tame the errant wisps that escape my braid, wishing I'd spent a little extra time putting myself together today. Never have I worried about such trivial things.

He rolls off, lying beside me on the ground, looking up at the stars overhead.

I refuse to think about who could be looking down to see this. I'm going to enjoy what little time I have left here with Luke, because it'll be the last time I see him. I know this can't happen again, no matter how badly I wish otherwise. I don't want to leave, and that's a very big problem.

His fingers graze mine, and I can't help but interlace mine with his. We lie there in the dark quiet of the night for what feels like hours. Words aren't necessary, as his touch tells me everything I need to know about the man beside me. He's gentle, capable of love, and he would be all mine if only it were possible.

As if sensing the direction of my wayward thoughts, he speaks, "I can't hide how I feel, Victoria. I want to know you better."

I huff. "That's impossible, Luke. It's forbidden for a reason."

He sits up, turning toward me. "What if I were to need your assistance again?"

I eye him skeptically. "Playing with fire."

Those piercing green eyes seem to dance. "For you, I'd walk right through it," he declares, leaning over me and placing a kiss on my temple. "Tell me I can see you again."

The answer is simple. No is the only word that should slip from my lips. We can't do this; it'll only bring trouble to both of us. If for no other reason, I need to protect him. But that's not what comes out.

"I-I'll try," I lie, knowing it's a promise I can't keep.

Luke frowns, as if he knows I'm simply placating him.

"Will you stay with me for a few more minutes?" he asks, sounding far away.

I squeeze his hand in answer, not wanting the moment to end. If I could stay forever, I would.

My eyes flutter open, and I sigh at the memory. Two nights in a row, Luke has commanded my dreams, and as much as I want to lie and say I hate it, I don't. A part of me will always crave him, because he wills it so. That's exactly why I need to keep Zeke at arm's length.

I roll to my side, taking in the sleeping form of the fallen angel next to me. His dark blond hair is matted to his forehead. My hand comes up and swipes the errant strands away, wishing I didn't have to complicate things.

"You're awake," his deep, groggy voice says with a hint of a smile to it.

"I had a nightmare."

It's not a complete lie. That memory might've been one to hold on to if it were anyone other than Luke it had been shared with.

"What's going on in that head of yours, pretty girl?"

I sigh. "Too heavy a conversation for this early in the morning," I admit wearily. "But one we definitely need to have soon."

Zeke props himself up on one elbow, looking down at me with concern. "Trust me, Tori. Tell me your secrets."

He has no idea what he's asking for. The truth will send him packing. He might've fallen, but my story is too much for even him to handle.

Trust him.

If I tell him and he runs away, then I can get back to life, hunting and being utterly alone. Or I could confide in someone for the first time, and maybe he'll understand. Maybe he'll still choose to stick around.

I don't say a word, lifting myself from the bed and heading to the single-serve coffee machine sitting on a desk in the corner. I'm not much of a coffee drinker, but every now and then it's necessary. This is one of those times. I can't make decisions about sharing my deepest secrets while I'm still half asleep. I can only hope it'll buy me time to think.

Thankfully, Zeke gives me the space I need, not saying a word. I go about making the coffee, carrying out the mundane steps needed to start the machine. All the while, I can feel his eyes burning a hole into my back. I don't dare turn around.

I stretch my arms up over my head, stretching out the kinks. Maybe I can distract him enough that once my coffee is done, the subject will be changed to sex. Seems like a great change.

"Tori." My name's drawn out in a scold as though Zeke read my mind. "Stop avoiding."

Luck is not on my side, apparently.

"I'm making coffee, Zeke. Can't you just be patient?" I call out over my shoulder, not actually making eye contact with him. I'm such a damn chicken.

He grunts but doesn't say another word, and for that I'm thankful.

The machine beeps, signaling my coffee's done and time's up. I take the piping-hot mug from under the dispenser and turn slowly. My eyes connect with Zeke and I take a sip, trying to buy myself even more time.

"Gah!" I screech as the entirety of the inside of my mouth is scorched from the far-too-hot liquid that's now spilling onto my hand. "Ahh!"

I slam the cup down on the counter, grabbing a rag and covering my hand.

"Come here," he says, motioning to the spot next to him.

My tongue moves across the roof of my burned mouth, feeling the bubbled top and wishing I hadn't been such an idiot.

"Tori. Come sit."

I expel a breath, making my way to the bed and taking a seat.

"Are you okay?" Zeke places his hand on my cheek, looking deeply into my eyes.

I sigh at his touch and the gentleness in his tone. No matter how far I try to run, he's always there to make me second-guess my actions. He's shown me in so many ways just how much he cares. He's the one person I can trust, and there's a large part of me begging to confess my sins to receive absolution.

Deciding to put my faith in Zeke, I take a deep breath and dive in.

"During a battle on Earth, I stumbled across a woman who was badly injured in the cross fire. There was a man with her." I pause, taking another breath, and forge ahead. "He asked me to intervene. He knew what I was, Zeke, and it didn't scare him."

"He asked you to save his wife?" Zeke's eyes are narrowed, giving away the fact he likely already knows the answer.

I shake my head. "They were together, but not . . . together. She was a single mom."

"So you helped her?"

"I did. But that's not even the worst of it. He asked my name, and I gave it to him."

Zeke's eyes widen. "Why would you do that? You know how serious that is."

"You're right. I did know. But it didn't stop me. I gave it willingly, and I only just barely regretted it." I tell the truth, because why lie? If I'm going to come clean, no sense in leaving out the minor details.

"Why didn't you care, Tori?"

I shrug. "I don't know. At least . . . I'm not sure why that first time didn't shake me."

"There were more times?"

I chew on my lip, not loving his accusatory tone.

"I'm sorry. I'm just . . . surprised."

"Yeah, well, it surprised me too."

"So, let me get this straight. You gave your name to a human, and he used it every time he found himself in harm's way."

"Sort of," I say, trying to skirt the whole truth. I'm not ready to divulge it all to him, despite my early confidence. His reactions have me backpedaling that notion. Baby steps.

"Sort of," he repeats.

"In truth, he only called out my name twice. Once was for help, and another was just to see me."

"Let me guess—the mortal fell for the angel," he said, lips turned up into a knowing smile. "Can't say I blame him."

I lower my head, feeling small under the weight of Zeke's

stare. He doesn't seem surprised or bothered by any of it, and that has me questioning what his story is.

Or I could just be satisfied that he's not running.

My conscience can be such a condescending brat.

"The question is, did you fall for him?"

It's the one question I knew he'd ask but hoped he wouldn't. Isn't it obvious? I fell from Heaven. For what other reason, given my story, would I choose that fate? This isn't him not knowing. This is him wanting me to say it out loud. Needing me to admit my greatest sin.

"Yes," I say, so quietly Zeke has to lean in to hear.

He whistles, and I glare at his reaction.

"I had my suspicions, but I never saw you being the type."

I bristle at his words. "The type?" I grate.

"Sweetheart, stop. I don't mean it like that. It's just you've always been such an independent woman. It's hard for me to hear that another man was enough to make you give everything up." He sits up, back against the headboard. "If I'm being honest, I hate that a guy had so much hold over you."

His deep frown and his arms crossed tightly over his chiseled chest give him away.

"You're jealous," I accuse, not able to mask my smile.

"Hell yes, I'm jealous."

I lean over and place a kiss on his mouth. "Trust me, the joke was on me."

Zeke relaxes, dropping his arms to his sides. "Will you tell me what happened?"

I groan but relent. "One night after I left him, I found Michael waiting for me back in Heaven. He dragged me in front of the council, and I was put on trial. They ruled that I gave my name. I argued it was given only under duress from the battle I'd just fought, and that the human had used it against me. They rejected my argument but spared me damnation. God stripped me of my rapier and banned me from fighting on Earth."

"Woah, that's . . . surprising. I'm shocked you weren't banished right then and there."

"If I had been one of the weaker angels, I probably would've been."

Zeke winced, and I realized my mistake. He was one of those weaker angels.

"I'm sorry, Zeke. I didn't mean it."

He shook his head. "Don't apologize for speaking truth, Tori." He may have waved off my apology, but his tone was laced with bitterness. "Tell me how you ended up falling."

I want to refuse based on his current mood, but instead, I allow the words to spill out.

"He was in danger and called my name. Having had it stripped from me, I didn't feel the pull to go because of other-worldly powers. This time, I chose it all on my own," I admit, lowering my head in shame. "I fell because I loved him, and I couldn't allow him to die."

"Love, then," Zeke says, a hint of sadness underlining his words.

"At that time, I thought so."

We sit in quiet contemplation for some time. I think back on all the moments that led up to that night. My brothers' stern talks after my trial, warning me to fear the fall. Looking back, it's almost like they knew it was inevitable but didn't attempt to sway me.

If only one of them had shaken me and forced me to see the truth that I had been missing. I was about to fall for someone who could never truly love me back.

Zeke feels miles away, and I wonder if I've just put myself in a similar situation. Zeke might want me, but love is something else entirely. It isn't an emotion that one chooses, knowing how harshly it can tear you apart when it's gone.

No matter what happens between Zeke and me, this time, it won't break me. That was already accomplished with the fall.

SUCKER FOR PAIN

Two days have gone by and I haven't seen hide nor hair of Zeke. When he left the loft the other day, he said he was going to round up his humans and get them caught up on the newest demons we encountered. He'd explained that he thought, given the events of the last time we were all together, the news would be better received if I wasn't there.

Two days is getting a bit excessive, and I can't help but feel like he's actually avoiding me. I trusted him with my secret—at least a good portion of it—because he asked me to. He can't be mad now. He fell too, and that means there isn't anything I've done that he can't rival. Liar.

I've spent the past two days taking my frustration out on the punching bag hanging from the barn rafters. Without knowing what else is roaming around out there, I haven't hunted. Fear isn't the issue. It's knowing when more training is needed. I have to be prepared, and storing energy is my preparation. Sure, I'll conjure another storm before we fight, but that's not something I can do every day. At some point, even in New Orleans, people would get suspicious.

In the meantime, I've been working on my strength. Starting by kicking the shit out of the bag again. I'm thirty minutes into my boxing workout when the sound of tires on the gravel alerts me to someone's approach—multiple someones. I grab a towel and wipe the sweat from my forehead, slinging the wet cloth onto a nearby chair.

Zeke saunters in, two hundred pounds of well-muscled angel. If he had shown up two days ago looking like this, I might've jumped him, but today . . . not a chance.

"Hey, baby," he croons, but I turn my back, effectively ignoring him.

He doesn't get to disregard me for two days and then show up here like everything is fine. Doesn't he know I've been questioning everything in his absence?

"Victoria," he calls, sounding mildly peeved at my less-than-hospitable behavior. "You're the one who chose a physical-only relationship."

Ass. Hole.

Throwing my own damn words back at me is low. Or fair. But that's something I won't admit out loud.

"You can't just ignore me."

"Wrong," I seethe.

I'm just about ready to tell him where he can go when I feel him at my back. His large hands come to my hips, pulling me back into his chest. His warm breath tickles my ears, and I try to repress the shiver it causes.

"You missed me that much?" he murmurs, and I turn to slap his chest.

"Don't try to be cute, Zeke. I'm pissed," I say, stalking off toward the loft stairs.

He catches me by the elbow, swinging me back toward him.

"Victoria, stop," he begs. "Let me speak."

I yank out of his grip, crossing my arms over my chest. It's as much permission as he's going to get.

"I did what we discussed. I rounded up the troops. They're here, ready to start training," he says, motioning toward the open barn door. "You don't get to have it both ways. This is either a friends-with-benefits situation or it's more. You choose, but you don't get both."

I hate him in this moment. Or more accurately, I hate his wise words and these damn human emotions swirling through me. It's confusing. Maddening. Awful.

Instead of acknowledging either choice, I turn back to the present situation. Humans are here and ready to fight.

"They're not going to get in my way?"

"Can't promise that. But they are trainable," Zeke says.

I suck my teeth before heading toward the driveway. Sure enough, a group of eager humans congregate around two additional trucks parked in the drive. Twice as many as Blaine's original group.

"Guys, meet Tori," Zeke says, saddling up beside me.

Names are rattled off in succession, but I hardly pay attention. I don't need to know their names; I need to know if they can fight. More importantly, I need to know if they can be trusted.

Humans are easily swayed by dark forces. If their lives are offered in exchange for their abandonment of our cause, they'll likely take it without a second thought. That doesn't make them evil; it makes them human. Which is exactly why I've never agreed to fight alongside them before.

"What are you fighting with?" I ask, hoping like hell none of them say their fists. If that's the answer, I'm going it alone.

A redhead with a face full of freckles steps forward. "Chad, ma'am. We've all worked with a coven—Dubai Coven of Savannah—to have blades, enchanted with angel rock, created."

My eyes shoot to Zeke's. I hope he can read my mind. What the actual hell. Humans working with witches? It appears the demons aren't the only ones sidling up to the covens.

"Did you organize this pact for them?" I direct my question toward Zeke. He grins in reply. "Did you discuss the current demon situation?"

"He did," Chad pipes up. "We're ready to train."

"You do realize that a hellhound was recently spotted," I press, wanting to gauge just how much Zeke has told them.

"Yes, ma'am," he drawls.

"And you understand that means Lucifer is on Earth?"

He nods. "We're prepared to die if it means saving the human race."

I huff, unconvinced that these men truly grasp the severity of Chad's declaration. Either way, it's their decision.

"Fine. Let's train," I say, walking back toward the barn with six humans lagging behind, none of which are Blaine and his crew.

"Who are these people?" I ask, as Zeke steps next to me. "Where's Blaine?"

"They're Savannah hunters. I met them last year. Blaine will be here. He needed some time to process everything."

I roll my eyes. "He's a pain in the ass."

Zeke chuckles. "That he can be."

We pair off, Zeke and I taking the lead. For over an hour, we practice fighting techniques, hand-to-hand combat and a cross between Muay Thai and judo.

I have to admit that the stamina and overall aptitude of the men is refreshing. A part of me had been convinced that they'd fall short, but Zeke was right. These men are skilled fighters.

Zeke and I are in a fighting sequence when he leans in and quietly says, "Are you going to admit I was right all along?"

My mouth forms a thin line, and I kick, trying to take out his feet. I miss, growling in frustration. I'm still miffed with Zeke, and his cocky attitude isn't helping. Based on his grin, he knows he's getting to me. I'm itching to wipe it off his face.

He takes advantage of my irritation and strikes back with his own kick. I fall heavily to my knees. My fists slam against the mat, anger rising at the fact that I was so distracted that I allowed him to take me down.

I spring to my feet, and we circle each other in crouched

positions. My black tank top hugs my curves and showcases the swell of my breasts. I press my arms to my sides, forcing my cleavage to pop. Zeke doesn't miss the protruding globes, and it's my turn to smirk, because he's officially distracted. He may be angelic, but not even that makes him immune to my female wiles.

I lunge forward, grabbing him by the neck and flipping over his body to bring him onto his back. I throw my legs over his chest so that I'm straddling him.

"How do you like that your human soldiers get to see you taken down by a girl?"

He leans up until our lips are just barely touching. "You're far from a simple girl, Tori," he says, nipping my bottom lip. "They've been warned not to underestimate you."

I smirk, but it doesn't last long. Zeke uses his weight to throw me off balance and onto my back, reversing positions with me.

"Have I told you how much I like having you underneath me?" he growls.

My frustration from earlier disappears, and suddenly a red-hot need sears me. I want him inside me.

"Head back to the hotel," he orders the men. "I'll see you tonight."

The humans don't stick around, chuckling as they make their way back to their trucks. They know full well what's coming next, and they're right to hightail it.

We don't wait for them to retreat. Zeke pulls me to my feet and lifts me into his arms. With our lips fused together, he carries me up the loft stairs.

"Need a shower," I murmur in between kisses.

In a matter of moments, I'm stripped naked and pressed against the shower wall, legs wrapped around Zeke's waist. His mouth lavishes a pert nipple, and a moan escapes my lips. My hands pull at his hair, desperation mounting.

"Please," I groan, begging for him to put me out of my misery.

Water cascades over us as he continues running one hand over the curves of my body, the other holding me in place.

"I missed you," he grunts. "Need you."

I nod my head, a silent plea for him to take what he wants. I'm frantic for the same thing. My nails rake down his back and it only seems to arouse him more. Without a word he slams up and into me. My head falls back, and my entire body comes alive at the feel of his thickness massaging my inside walls.

I bask in the pleasure, thanking whoever is listening for this moment. Why did I avoid it for so long? Nothing has ever felt this good. Every single touch has me feeling more alive than I ever have before. A future may not be in our cards, but this right here—I'm down for it.

After multiple rounds, we both collapse in my bed, sated and exhausted.

"That," he starts, then stops, causing me to smirk into his shoulder.

"Was incredible?" I offer.

"Beyond," he admits.

"I promised the boys we'd hunt tonight, but I'll admit, I don't know that my legs will work." He chuckles.

"We have to," I say, wishing like hell we could stay put. "It's one thing fighting each other, but we need to rid the world of more demons."

He kisses me long and hard. "Promise me you'll be careful tonight," he requests, and I narrow my eyes.

"I've been fighting demons since I fell, Zeke. Nothing has changed."

"Everything has changed," he snarls, kissing me roughly this time. "You're finally mine and I won't lose you, Tori."

His words are sobering. I have enjoyed everything we've shared and yes, I might be softening to the idea of more with Zeke, but he's ten steps ahead. We can't really move forward until I've told him the whole truth, and even then, I'm not sure I can allow myself to open my heart completely again.

His phone rings, saving me from having yet another argument about this pseudo-relationship. I listen to his clipped discussion that lasts for all of two minutes.

"Zombies have been spotted just off Jackson Square."

"Zombies?" I yelp.

"Get ready. We need to go."

I spring from the bed, locating my hunting gear. All the while I'm replaying his words in my head. Demons, werewolves, hellhound, and now zombies. War is brewing, and as much as I don't want to admit it, we aren't prepared.

BAD BLOOD

A HORDE of zombies slink through the dark alleys two blocks from Jackson Square. Our group has managed to trap them between two deserted parking lots, away from humans, and a ward has been put in place to keep the area free from passersby.

On the way over, we divided ourselves into groups of three. Chad—the apparent leader of the Savannah group—leads one, and Zeke and I manage the others.

Zeke's team, comprised of Charlie and Joe, appears to be the weakest of the Savannah crew, but they're still light-years ahead of where I thought they'd be. With some training, they'll be very useful.

This leaves me and the remaining two humans, John and Tyler, to take on the last group. It's clear that Zeke left me with the two most competent mortals as they swing their blades overhead and crash into one zombie after another, barely breaking a sweat. They're even able to help Zeke's crew with the remaining zombies.

I'm almost disappointed that they don't need me. I live for the fight, and being sidelined isn't sitting well, but they need the practice more than I do. So I lean against the wall, bored and ready for this to end. Zombies are easy to exterminate.

Chad and Ethan almost have our lot cleared when a raucous noise sounds from the old cemetery bordering the abandoned spot.

"Can you handle this?" I yell to Tyler, who nods in return.

I'm making my way toward the gates of the cemetery when the noise escalates to a fever pitch.

"What the hell," I say out loud, scanning the area, coming up empty-handed.

The ground shakes, and slits in the ground open up to holes where bodies were likely buried. It's then that I put the pieces together.

The zombies are being risen from the grave.

Only one being is capable of such atrocities—a necromancer. If corpses are being exhumed from the ground, the city is in deep trouble. There is no way that Zeke and I, with our band of misfit humans, can stop whatever voodoo is being enacted.

"Victoria," a familiar voice calls from behind. I don't need to turn to know who it is. I should've known something this dire for Earth would bring them.

"Leeanna," I reply. "Glad you finally saw fit to intervene."

She lets out a humorless laugh. "I'm surprised you care. I thought your fall from grace would have you preoccupied with other things."

Her voice is laced with venom, but I don't have time to analyze the angel's issues. I knew that my first run-in with my past would be awkward at best and painful at worst. Right now, despite the issues between us, we need to work together.

She stands beside me, surveying the scene. The dead are crawling from their crypts at a snail's pace. The one nice thing about zombies is that they're painfully slow-moving.

"Can I trust you?" Leeanna snarls, and I roll my eyes.

"I trained you, and fallen or not, I could still kick your ass." She bristles at my words but nods her head once.

"For the sake of Earth, I'll allow you to fight with me." I want to growl and shake her until her wings molt, but there are more pressing matters than revenge on my traitorous ex-sister-in-arms.

I pull Solis from my back and prepare to fight.

It's a bloodbath as additional angels fall from the sky, joining the battle. Our swords slice through the air, lopping off heads and severing limbs. The zombie bodies fall in heaps to the ground. One by one, we take them out until none are left and the cemetery is littered with the decomposing carcasses.

I wipe Solis clean, basking in the afterglow of an intense fight.

"Wipe the smile off your face, traitor," Malachi sneers, and I inhale deeply, willing myself to calm down.

I brought their hatred on by my own actions. I know this, yet it doesn't stop me from wanting to challenge each and every one of the angels currently glaring at me. I just helped them; couldn't they just leave me in peace?

"Leave her alone, Mal," Leeanna chides, and I am just about to thank her when she continues, "She's filth."

I growl, stalking toward her.

"Careful, traitor. We can end you with one blow of our blades," Malachi threatens.

"Fair fight," I snap. "You and I both know, with my blade, you don't stand a chance."

"You lost that the day you decided to be a deserter," Leeanna says, sounding tired and bored.

"Victoria." Zeke's anxious voice carries across the cemetery, drawing all of our attention. I don't miss the way Leeanna stiffens.

"Over here," I call out.

When he rounds the corner, his eyes are trained on me. He jogs up, crashing me into his chest and slamming his lips to mine. A choked sound has us pulling apart. Zeke's eyes lift and land on the trio of archangels. He jumps back, eyes wide.

"Lee," he says, and I narrow my eyes.

Nobody has ever called Leeanna *Lee*. Pet names are reserved for mortals, not angelic beings. He's on Earth and emotions run high down here. Anything he once felt in Heaven is amplified tenfold.

Zeke had a thing for Leeanna.

She doesn't reply to him; instead, her heated glare finds mine, and not even a second later, she pounces, sending us both flying back into a mausoleum. We roll several times before I gain the upper hand, pressing her shoulders into the ground roughly.

My hand rises and is on its way down to smack against her porcelain face when someone yanks me from her. I spin on my feet, ready to tackle Malachi for interfering, when I realize it's Zeke who stopped me.

"Don't," he warns. "You know what the punishment is for assaulting an angel."

"It's too late for that," Malachi derides. "I'm taking her life."

He stalks toward me, grabbing my arms and holding them behind my back, sending a searing pain through my shoulders. I cry out at the intense burn.

"You can't," Zeke barks. "Look around. These demons won't stop coming. You need us on the ground. Unless you want God sending you here for however long is necessary."

Leeanna balks.

"You're in no position to barter, traitor," Malachi jeers at Zeke, throwing the same insult at him.

"Lee," Zeke pleads, "you know I'm right."

"Are you? Plans change all the time."

"What game are you playing?" he snaps.

"Why do you care what happens to her?" Her lip lifts into a Cheshire-cat grin that looks more evil than angelic. Her reaction belies her words. She's mocking him. But for what exactly? "You already know the ending."

I'd still be considering what the hell she's talking about if Zeke's reaction hadn't caught my attention. His back is straight, and his eyes are narrowed on Leeanna.

"What is she talking about?" I ask, looking between the two.

"Why, Lee? After everything?"

Despite the fact that I'm moments away from having my life snuffed out at the hands of my former friends, I'm jealous. Pain, regret, and something akin to yearning radiates off both Leeanna and Zeke. My Zeke.

I don't want anything serious. He's not mine.

"Burn her, for all I care," Lee says, before turning her back on all of us and walking away.

"You coward," I scream at her retreating form, as Malachi lowers me to my knees, securing my hands together behind my back.

"Any last words?" he says through gritted teeth.

"This is done, Mal. You and I both know this joke has gone too far." Zeke's glare is lethal.

"Has it?"

Zeke doesn't get to say another word as something large crashes through the cemetery, taking down tombstones as it runs toward us. Malachi's head lifts to the sky and he wails, a sound that makes my ears feel like they're going to bleed. I can't even shield them from the sound, since my hands are still secured behind me.

The crashing continues. It's getting closer. Malachi and the others spread their wings before they all take to the skies, retreating. As soon as they are out of sight, the loud sound ceases.

Zeke and I share an ominous look. The cemetery is eerily quiet. Not a single bird chirps or branch rustles. The wind that once whipped through this place is gone. If the lack of noise isn't odd enough, the bigger question is what could've frightened off three archangels?

"Victoria."

The word is whispered in my ear for only me to hear. Chills cascade over my body, leaving me cold to the bone.

Lucifer.

He's here, and that is not good for me.

When we're back at the loft, Zeke holds me in his arms and strokes my hair. I haven't stopped shaking since the cemetery.

"Baby, you're safe," Zeke coos in my ear. "They were just playing a horrible prank."

If only that were the reason for my trembling.

"Angels don't prank, Zeke." My teeth chatter. The cold that slipped under my skin is bone deep and not retreating, no matter how many blankets he layers me with.

"On Earth they do." He inhales. "They won't get away with anything like that again."

They being Leeanna and Malachi. Two angels who at one time were my family. We had each other's backs. Now, they'd throw me to the wolves. The sequence of the night's events runs through my head and keeps getting stuck on the interaction between Zeke and Leeanna. So many strange comments and looks of longing. I might never unsee them.

I'm torn between wanting Zeke here and wanting him far away from me. He came to my defense, but his affection for Leeanna is clear to anyone with half a brain. With that thought, the chills subside and give way to a burning anger. An unfair anger.

"Are you going to tell me what was up between you and *Lee*?" I say her name with disdain I can't help.

Not only were we once friends, but I'd been her mentor. Didn't that count for something? I didn't fall to betray her. I fell because I was duped. She's an angel; she surely knows the entire sordid story.

"We were in the same legion," Zeke starts, sounding resigned to this conversation but disinclined nonetheless. "We went to Earth often, and each time we were there our feelings . . . ," he says through his teeth, as though the admission hurts, "grew."

I puff out my cheeks, wondering how the heck that worked once they got back to Heaven, and he doesn't disappoint, moving right into that topic.

"When we'd return, things went back to normal, for the most part. But with each trip back to Earth, when we returned, a little bit of those feelings came back too." He runs a hand down his face. "We decided to fall together," he admits, and my mouth forms an O in surprise at this turn of events. "Needless to say, I fell, and she didn't."

"Oh. Wow," I say, processing this news. "Let me make sure I understand this," I say, not trying to come off as hoity-toity, but truly wanting to understand. "You fell in love with an angel, decided to fall together, and when the time came you did, and she chose to let you fall without following."

I want to push and nag for more sordid details, because that's my current mental state, self-sabotage. Zeke doesn't allow it, pushing forward and making it clear the entire conversation has him vexed.

"That pretty much sums it up," he says.

"I'm sorry, Zeke. That's . . . awful."

I mean every word. I don't like it, but I care for him. He was as duped into falling as I was, and it isn't fair. Add to it that he's still harboring feelings for her, and that just plain sucks. The truth is, I get it. We both have a past hanging over our heads. Unfinished business has a way of sticking around and screwing with your life. I get that more than anyone. Case in point, my dreams as of late.

Having witnessed Zeke and Leeanna's whole reunion, it was obvious the feelings were not one-sided, but I'm not about to point that out. Maybe that makes me selfish—definitely makes me selfish—but I'm going to hang on to the one thing that is looking up for me here on Earth. God can deal with Leeanna. I need to help Zeke move on.

"I don't want to talk about Lee or the past. I just want you," he says, burying his head in my hair. "I freaked out when I couldn't find you."

"I'm fine," I say, snuggling into him. "I'm badass, remember?"

He chuckles. "That you are, babe. A total badass."

We both laugh, falling into our own comfortable silence, until Zeke breaks it with the one question I was hoping to avoid.

"What do you think scared off the arcs?"

Saying his name is the equivalent of summoning him, and nobody wants that. Plus, I'm exhausted and don't want to discuss the events of tonight.

"I don't know. But I'm grateful," I lie, to steer us in another path.

"Me too," he says, rolling on top of me, effectively ending all conversation.

His lips press against mine, begging entry, and I willingly open to him. Our tongues caress, and a moan escapes my mouth. Zeke's large hands grab my hips, switching our positions. I giggle at the sudden change-up, but stop short when I look down into lust-filled eyes that belong to someone other than Zeke.

Luke.

I gasp, scrambling back.

"Tori, what's wrong?"

Zeke's voice.

My head snaps up, and this time, it's Zeke staring back at me in equal parts confusion and concern.

"I . . . uh. I thought—" My head shakes back and forth as I try to formulate words and calm my racing heart. "I thought I saw something. A spider." I tack the last part on to try to explain my reaction.

Zeke frowns, likely seeing through my lie, but he doesn't call me on it. Instead, he pats the bed beside him, motioning for me to come back and lie down. I crawl up the bed and snuggle under the covers, head tipped to the ceiling.

Why did I see Luke in that moment? Why has he been on my mind at all? The frequency is increasing, and with all the shit happening around us, a coincidence seems doubtful. Falling for him brought me to Earth to face all this shit.

"Tori, look at me," Zeke commands. My head turns wearily in his direction, but I don't say anything. "Whatever's going on, we'll get through it. You don't have to shoulder the burdens alone. We're all in this."

I sigh heavily. "I don't know if we'll be enough, Zeke. What's coming . . . it's bigger than us. I can feel it."

He pulls me in to his side, resting his head against mine. "God won't allow it. He'll intervene."

"That doesn't change the fact that the casualties will be great, Zeke. You know it."

"I do, but let's not focus on that tonight. I want you in my arms."

"I'm in your arms." I chuckle, despite the major shift in subject matter. No matter how necessary of a conversation the upcoming battle is, tonight, it can wait.

"Then maybe I want you under my body instead."

"Now that, I can get on board with."

He shifts so he's back on top, kissing the base of my neck.

"Yes," I whimper. "Keep doing that."

He doesn't obey, instead moving down my body, lifting my shirt to continue placing kisses across my stomach. I squirm under his touch, but don't dare move.

"Sit up," he commands, and I do.

He removes my shirt and bra in one move, leaving my chest bare and at his disposal. His mouth wraps around one nipple, nipping and sucking. It feels so good. Good enough to distract my mind from wandering to places I don't want to go.

After the night we had, I plan to get lost in the comfort that only Zeke can offer. No more thoughts of Luke and demons. Right now, in Zeke's arms, I'm going to bask in the pleasure he's providing.

YOU'RE SOMEBODY ELSE

My back slams against the cold concrete building in a dark alley outside of the bar we just left.

A bar. Who am I even?

Luke's tongue begs entrance to my mouth, and I give it willingly, moaning in response to his expert abilities. I don't want to even think about how much experience he's had to provoke such pleasure.

Luke holds my hips pressed against him as his tongue massages mine. I love the feeling. All of the intense emotions felt here on Earth are overwhelming. Every touch I feel to my bones. Every kiss sends my stomach free-falling. I'm on the verge of tears and I have absolutely no idea why. Pure joy is the only explanation I have.

This night is everything I never thought I needed but wouldn't be without now that I've experienced it. It's been all I hoped for. What I fell for.

We spent the night dancing, bodies pressed tightly together, our lips fused, cementing our budding relationship.

Budding. I laugh to myself. We're so far past that. It's as if I've known Luke my entire life. He makes me feel things that I never thought possible.

"I'm never letting you go, Victoria." He says my name like

a prayer, and butterflies take flight in my belly at the reverence in his voice. "I'm going to love you until the day I die," he vows, and I smile, feeling his words in my soul, because I feel the same way.

The hairs on the back of my neck stand erect, signaling danger is close by. Apparently, there are some things that even falling can't take from me. Demon radar being one of them.

"What's wrong?" he whispers, placing a kiss on the curve of my neck.

"Something's coming. Something dangerous," I explain, and he doesn't appear bothered in the least.

"It'll be fine, Victoria. Stay here with me," he croons.

The certainty in his voice and my eagerness to please him has me relinquishing my concern and giving myself over to him for safekeeping.

I'm lost in the feel of his hands wandering my body when I'm jerked out of his grasp. My body is hurled toward the ground, and I smack hard into the asphalt of the alley floor. When I look up, two glowing red eyes meet mine. Feral and out for blood.

A demon.

I scramble back, unsure what defenses I still possess. I just fell this afternoon, and I lost my blade in the process. A feeling of absolute helplessness invades my troubled mind. How can I save us?

Internally, I berate myself. I'm still a celestial being. That's something that not even the fall can take away from me. These creatures have crumbled under my touch for centuries. While I'm busy psyching myself up for this fight, the demon lunges toward me, dagger in hand.

I yell out, curling into a ball, trying to protect myself, but the impact I expect never comes. My arms fall to my sides, and when I look up, dread fills me completely. The air is sucked from my lungs and my heart stops.

"Luke?" my voice wavers, eyes opening and closing, trying desperately to unsee what's laid out before me.

Luke—my Luke—is hovering off the ground, a pair of raven wings protruding from his back. His eyes are the color of night, and his face is twisted in a menacing glare that has even the demon cowering. In a voice unrecognizable to me, he instructs the demon to go back to Hell, and it obeys. Its head lowers and it slinks into the shadows, reprimanded and submissive.

Luke's gaze turns to me and I know.

"Lucifer."

My hands fly to my mouth, covering my pathetic moan of guilt and betrayal.

"Victoria."

My head shakes back and forth violently as my hands cover my ears to drown out his deceitful words. Never allow the devil to whisper in your ear; you'll fall victim every time. I'm proof of that.

With a flutter of his wings, he disappears, leaving me alone in the alley.

I curl back into a ball, weeping, praying to God to end my existence.

His mercy never comes.

Zeke's phone blares to life from the nightstand, jarring us both.

The memory of the night I fell makes me sick. I fly from the bed, falling to my knees at the base of the toilet, spilling the contents of my stomach. I heave as my diaphragm clenches. Bile trickles from my lips.

I've repressed the truth for so long. Luke was Lucifer in disguise. The ultimate trickster convinced me to fall in the false name of love. The reminder of my idiocy has me hurling into the porcelain god again. When I think I'm finished, I lay my cheek against the lid and try to get my racing heart under control.

As much as I want to come clean to Zeke, I'm not ready. I haven't admitted to anyone that I fell for the devil.

"What?" Zeke's hard tone filters into the bathroom, drawing my attention and giving my mind a short reprieve. "I'll be there within the hour. Be ready," he says, before everything goes quiet.

I stand, making my way to the sink. Looking in the mirror, I cringe at my reflection. Clammy skin and an ashen complexion stare back at me. My hands press into the cold counter as I continue to inspect my face. Oh, how the mighty have fallen. A once beloved angel of Heaven has been reduced to a sick-looking girl, hardly fit to walk Earth. I want to scream at the top of my lungs. I want to rage at Lucifer for making me this pathetic girl.

What would that accomplish?

I grab a towel from the counter and wipe my mouth roughly, then quickly brush my teeth and swish with mouthwash. All to buy myself some time to pull it together. When my body is finally done shaking, I walk back to meet Zeke.

"Are you okay?"

"Fine. My stomach is just a bit queasy. No big deal." I try to brush it off, but Zeke's narrowed gaze tells me he's not buying it. "Where are you going?" I push forward, sounding tired and weak.

"Blaine's group has more questions. They showed up here last night, but we were already gone. I need to fill them in on what happened in the cemetery. It's likely we'll encounter arcs again." He purses his lips in thought. "They need to know the whole truth."

I sigh. "Do you think there will be repercussions from Heaven for telling them?"

He runs his palms over his face. "We're going to need more than two fallens to take on whatever's coming, Tori. What other choice do we have? The archangels are inconsistent with their help. We can't rely on them. We'll all die anyway."

103

I hate to admit that he's right. Whatever war is upon us, we'll need all hands on deck. The human men have proven to be decent allies, but will they be enough?

"Leeanna barely allowed me to fight next to her. What do you think she'll do if humans get involved?"

"I'm not worried about Lee. She'll do what's best for Heaven and Earth."

"You have that much faith in her after everything?" The edge in my voice seems to strike a nerve. Zeke's eyes darken and his lips form a hard, straight line.

"We're not talking about Lee, Tori."

My teeth clench and my hands ball into fists. The need to rage is so intense that I can feel my face heating with all the pent-up anger. Inhaling and then exhaling, I bring myself under control. It's not only this conversation that has me ready for a fight. My dream is playing a key role, and because of it, I don't want to go down this path. It's not relevant to the issue at hand.

"I think it's time we start looking for other fallen angels."

Zeke groans. "There are none. I've looked."

His total disregard for my suggestion does nothing but reenergize my ire.

"Maybe they're better at hiding than you are."

He turns on me, red-faced and completely unlike Zeke. "Why am I never good enough for you, Tori?"

"W-what?" I ask, slinking backward, trying to put as much distance as possible between us. Zeke's reaction to a simple statement is so unlike him. The day has gone downhill ever since the mention of Leeanna's name, and I have to question why. Why does the mention of her elicit such an intense negative reaction, still?

"I never said that," I say, voice rising to meet his.

"You might as well. You insinuate it all the fucking time." He takes two giant steps toward me, and I step backward in response.

My hands come up to forestall his advance. "Please stop. You're scaring me."

His glare retreats, regret left in its place. "I'm so sorry. I didn't mean—"

"Is this all because I mentioned Leeanna?" The question is asked before I can consider whether I really want the confirmation. I already know, but hearing him say it will sting even more.

He grimaces, and that confirms it. "Don't bother," I say, turning my back and bending to retrieve my shirt. I pull it over my head, shielding my nakedness from Zeke, needing the armor.

"Tori, please. I'm struggling."

My hands come to my hips. "You're struggling? From what, Zeke?"

"Everything," he grates. "Your reason for falling. Our run-in with the arcs."

"You've got to be kidding me. Now you want to bring up my reason for falling? How about you just admit the damn truth?" I spit the words. "Let's not sugarcoat what really has you all bent. This is all about your feelings for Lee."

His face falls, and a small portion of my anger disintegrates at the look of utter self-loathing in his eyes. "My feelings for you are . . ." He runs his hands roughly through his hair, which I'm coming to find is a habit of his. "It's intense. I don't know how to handle it. It's more than what I ever felt for her."

"Don't," I say, shaking my head and grinding my teeth. "Don't pretend this is about you and me."

His shoulders slacken and tears—freaking *tears*—well in his eyes. I don't know how to handle this side of Zeke. I've only ever known the strong hunter. The relentless pursuer. The intense lover. This side of him is something entirely foreign.

"It's everything, Tori. Since I fell, there were only two emotions plaguing me. Lust and anger. Since you came into the picture, it's so much more. It's suffocating me."

"More? What more is there?"

"Love, Tori. I fucking love you."

I stagger back at his admission. Our physical arrangement just began. Love? That's out of the damn question.

The lust and anger I get, but love? No matter how many years we've spent on Earth, the range of emotion that's been foreign to us for centuries is hard to control at times. When you've gone lifetimes not feeling a thing, being on Earth can be overwhelming and all-consuming. Especially when you feel everything so acutely.

"Don't look at me like that," Zeke lectures. "You don't get to pretend that you don't feel something more for me. You practically took my head off for being away for two damn days, Tori. You obviously care."

I do. I care a lot. There's no questioning that. It's the love part that has me speechless. I've only felt a strong pull to someone one other time, and it was all a farce. It's hard for me not to question my own feelings when they've failed me so epically in the past.

"Whatever this is," I say, gesturing between the two of us, "it's something. But love? I'm not even sure I know what that feels like."

He takes a giant step toward me, grabbing my hands in his. "I'm not asking for you to love me back. Not yet. I only want you to be open to it."

My heart swells at the sincerity and hopefulness I see in Zeke. It gives me faith that my days on Earth can be so much more than I ever dreamed. I can build a life here. One to be proud of, despite what Heaven thinks. Maybe those thoughts are Earth making me foolish, but I'm not going to question it. Almada said I have a new path, and damn it, I'm going to be the one to forge it. At least the parts I can.

"One day, I might be open to it." I say, drawing the widest smile from Zeke.

He picks me up, swinging me around. I chuckle at the sensation, all the while instructing him to put me down. When

I'm placed back down on wobbly legs, he places a kiss on my mouth and whispers, "You'll love me one day."

He pulls me back onto the bed, into his strong arms, searing me with a kiss that makes me lightheaded.

"You've got it bad, Kincaid."

"You have no idea," he growls into my lips, and I smile, loving that for now, he's mollified. Thoughts of his feelings for Leeanna have disappeared for the moment.

I kiss him harder, savoring the energy that flows between us. If we were both powered up, I'd deepen our connection and light the damn sheets on fire. To prove whatever is building between us is worth more than whatever he had with Lee. It's ridiculous and childish, but it can't be helped.

He groans. "I have to go. I won't be long."

"Stay," I beg, knowing full well he can't. Something is brewing, and we need to be in front of it. Getting the humans ready is important.

"Think you can whip up a storm today?"

I smirk. "Hail and all?"

"The bigger, the better," he says, placing one last kiss on my mouth. "I need to recharge, and so do you."

"I'll work on it."

I finish getting dressed while Zeke does the same. I'm pulling my Nikes on when he speaks.

"Tori, I know you're still thinking about Lee, but you know that's over, right? I've proven that you're it for me, haven't I?"

After what I witnessed last night, I couldn't deny that a very large part of me knows he's not being honest with himself. A larger part wants to believe that his reaction was only to her randomly showing up. I'd have the same reaction if it were Luke.

"I do," I say, knowing that it doesn't matter either way, because there is no chance for Lee and Zeke given their stations. He fell and she stayed.

Right now, heavy conversations aren't a good idea. I need levity. I need to get back to the flirtatious camaraderie we had going before we took the nose-dive into Leeanna territory.

Self-preservation kicks in out of nowhere, and I'm standing up straighter, fixing my hair—for some ridiculous reason—and taking a deep breath to change tack. I won't allow myself to go down this tragic road of pathetic.

"I know you're mine. I was just hoping we could cement that fact by spending more time in bed." I go for his jugular. I've already stooped to insecure—might as well run the gamut to seductive. Why the hell not. Seems like a good time to let my feelings take me on a wild ride to crazy town.

He grunts. "I've waited for two years for you to say that, and I'm not even able to bask in my winnings."

Much to my surprise, I'm feeling better already. I make a mental note to look for a therapist. ASAP.

"I was also kind of hoping for round two of shower sex," I continue to goad, unexpectedly emboldened.

"You're killing me, English."

"Angels don't have last names."

"We're playing at mortal, babe. Last names are essential here."

"And you went with Kincaid?"

"It's a strong name. Ezekiel Kincaid."

I giggle at his territorial attitude about his name. As sad as it is, it makes me feel wanted to have him spend his time talking to me. It's inane, but it's something I've never had. A companion. Someone to just shoot the shit with. Zeke has become that person for me. The one I want to share silly news with and spill my deepest secrets to. With the uncertainties I'm feeling, his absence will be felt twice as acutely when he finally leaves. I don't want him to go.

Good grief, I'm pitiful.

From the giggle that's far more girly than tolerable to the flip-flopping moods, it's becoming clear that Earth has made me a mess.

Who am I even?

"When I get back, we're staying in bed for days if we can." Zeke's voice brings me back to the conversation at hand. "Ordering food and watching a boatload of movies too."

He grins. "Wouldn't have it any other way, angel."

I flinch at the moniker, and thankfully he doesn't notice. It's what Luke had called me, and the thought leaves sourness behind.

"I'll be back in an hour or so." He places one last kiss to my cheek before leaving me to myself in the loft.

That nickname has me thinking about things I have no business thinking about. Not after everything Zeke just shared with me. I need a shower, and then I need to drum up a storm to revive my powers. The need to run is intense but eclipsed by the thought of running into Lucifer. He was near. I could feel him.

I'm not ready to face the king of the damned. Somehow, I managed to escape the hound unscathed the last time I ran the trails, and I'm not about to press my luck.

Lucifer spared me.

I shiver at that reality. It's the only explanation. Hellhounds don't show mercy unless given direct orders. He also scared off the archangels. No matter how badly I want to dissect that, I have work to do. Satan, Lucifer, king of Hell, Luke—whatever the heck you want to call him—would only bask in the idea that I am thinking of him.

The master of deception, epitome of evil. Not someone I'll give another single thought to. It would only give him power over me.

If he spared me, he'll come to collect his favor.

I punch my pillow, irate that I have allowed myself to be in such a position. It's the truth, and I damn well know it. When Lucifer saves your life, he comes calling. He is the bargainer, and my life has been spared for a price, whether I asked for it or not.

I have to be ready for him.

THEREFORE I AM

THE HAIL COMES FIRST, beating into my bared skin, melting instantly on contact. I allow the heavy rain to drench me through. My hands come up over my head, calling upon the clouds to form the cyclone that'll deliver the energy I desperately need. My skin tingles with the knowledge that any moment, my call will be answered.

My eyes close in preparation, but the wind never comes. Baffled, I open my eyes to realize the clouds aren't obeying. The sky is the correct shade of green, but nothing twirls above. In fact, everything is entirely too still.

There's only one being that could interfere with my God-given gifts—another angel. A powerful one at that.

"Where are you?" I call out, head swiveling left to right, trying to pinpoint where the angel is hiding out. What's their motive for being here? I crouch low, getting into a fighting stance. I won't be blindsided by an attack.

"Very perceptive, Victoria." Leeanna's voice sounds from overhead. I turn to see her loitering on a tree branch. She leaps into the air, but her descent to the ground is slow and graceful. "Glad to see one thing about you hasn't been corrupted."

"What do you want?" I growl. The last encounter we had almost ended badly for me, and I haven't forgotten that.

She shrugs. "I came to have a chat with an old friend."

"I'm not your friend. Tell me what you want and get the hell off my property."

Her eyes light up. "I see pleasantries aren't necessary. I was afraid I'd have to go through this whole conversation playing at friends. I really don't have time to fake anything, so I'll cut to the chase."

"You have two minutes to state your business before I remove you myself."

She laughs. "You can't possibly think you can still take me. Those days are over."

"It might not be as easy as it once was, but I won't go down easily. Even you aren't dumb enough to think otherwise."

"I have God on my side."

"I don't, so there's nothing stopping me from ending your existence. Or at least trying. I can assure you I'll take extra care in making sure it's excruciatingly painful."

Leeanna takes a menacing step forward, baring her teeth. "Careful, Tori. God might have plans for you, but if you get in my way, I'll end you."

Now it's my turn to laugh. "You? Disobey God? You don't have the nerve."

"Try me."

"You're still his obedient little minion. Nothing more. You and I both know that if he wills me to live, you're powerless over it." I shrug. "Unless you've decided to fall after all."

"After all?" Her eyes narrow in what appears to be confusion.

"Zeke told me about your plans. Pretty shitty of you to lead him to believe you'd ever actually think for yourself."

"What are you talking about?"

"We're playing that game now? Trying to act as though you aren't the reason Zeke's stuck here?"

She shakes her head, looking thrown off balance more than anything. "You have no idea what you're talking about."

"Don't I? I know that you act all high and mighty, judging me for falling victim to the king of deceit, but you won't even admit that you yourself caused an angel to fall by tricking him into thinking you loved him."

She jerks back, her reaction switching from stunned to pissed. "Is that what he told you? That I made him fall?" She laughs incredulously. "You really are daft, Victoria. No wonder you were duped by Satan so easily."

"What the hell do you want?" I scream, causing a nearby flock of birds to shoot into the sky, scared off by my sudden outburst. Even Lee's eyes widen.

"I came to warn you."

I huff. "Why should I believe that you'd ever offer any word of warning to me? Am I not the scum on the bottom of your shoe? Or whatever it was you said about me back in the graveyard."

"I might've been unfair."

"Unfair?" I screech. "You have no idea what I've been through. You can't even fathom the kind of game that was played on me." I let the anger fester, unwilling to go easy on her. Not after she turned her back on me. "I didn't stand a chance." I choke on the words, desperately needing air.

Leeanna used to be one of my closest confidantes, but now, the sight of her makes me sick. She turned her back on me the first opportunity she had, never once asking why or trying to understand my point of view. She's the worst kind of backstabber.

"I get it. I was struggling with my own emotions being back on Earth. I was harsh. Too harsh." She blows out a breath. "I'm not asking you to forgive me, but I came with an olive branch."

"Why should I believe you?"

"You probably shouldn't." Leeanna's head falls, resigned.

"But I came nonetheless, with a warning and a potential solution."

"Go on." It's all I can muster. I don't trust her, but I won't squander the opportunity for information if for some reason she is actually here to deliver relevant information.

"There's a coup going down in the underground, and it'll take all of God's legions to stop it from coming to fruition. The humans that Zeke has aligned himself with are not mere humans."

My ears perk up at this news. What can that possibly mean?

"They're Nephilim."

I gasp. "Nephilim? They're real?"

She nods. "Yes, and we need them to come into their full power. It's imperative to this battle being won by Heaven."

"But they're forbidden celestial beings. God himself is said to have snuffed them out of existence when he learned of their existence. How is this possible?"

Leeanna's head swivels as though she's searching the area for eavesdroppers. "That's what angels are told to prevent us from acting on the human instincts that assault us when we come to Earth. Kind of like the whole Bible thing. It's more of a tale to keep us in line as opposed to absolute truth."

"So he doesn't exterminate Nephilim? What about the angels that created them? Are they roaming Earth too?"

Her hands shoot up to stop my assault of questions. "I don't know everything. You know Heaven's rules. We only know what we need to know where Earth is concerned."

I roll my eyes. Such antiquated ideals. If we're to protect humans and Heaven, isn't it vital to have all of the information? Is it smart to allow one entity to hold so much power? Not once has a single angel questioned God's motives behind these blatant censorships.

Lucifer did.

"They need to be trained differently, Victoria. They're celestial, and they are capable of so much more than what you've seen. Knowing this, you need to lead their training. You're the only one here on Earth worthy of such a task."

"What about Zeke? Shouldn't you be confiding in your former almost-lover?"

Leeanna grunt. "You and I both know Ezekiel was never as strong as you. You're the best to lead this earthly legion." She pulls her bottom lip into her mouth and seems to consider her next words. "For the record, we weren't lovers. Almost or otherwise. You got a distorted version of things. Why he's lying to you, I have no idea, but he isn't telling you the truth."

I search Leeanna's face for some tell that she's the one lying, but I find nothing but honesty in what she's saying. If nothing else, she certainly believes things went down differently.

"Your Zeke is hiding things, Victoria. You don't have to believe me, but you shouldn't blindly trust him either. If we're to defeat Hell's army, we need to all put our differences aside and be honest with each other. God might not want you to have all the answers, but truly, I think you deserve to know everything."

"Which is?" I press, wanting to end the riddles and get to the deception she's alluding to.

"That's a conversation that needs to be had with Ezekiel."

She might not be lying about the secrets, but I know Leeanna has ulterior motives. She always does. I just need to uncover what her intentions are.

"What conversation is that, Lee?" Zeke's deep timbre has me spinning to see him walking with purpose toward us. His eyes are trained on her, fire burning behind his irises. He's pissed, and all his anger is directed at her.

Maybe there is hope that he'll get over her after all.

"I'm only trying to clear up some misunderstandings that you seem to have created between Victoria and me. She seems to be under the impression that I jilted you. Why is that, Ezekiel?"

"I'm not speaking about the conversations I have with Tori to you. You aren't part of our relationship."

"Seems you're building said relationship on lies, or at the least half-truths."

The growl that rips through Zeke's chest has my eyebrows shooting skyward, but Lee doesn't so much as balk.

"Leave," he seethes.

She smirks, turning to face me. "Good luck, Victoria. Remember what I said."

With that last reminder of her warning, she shoots into the sky, leaving me to deal with a very hostile Zeke.

"What was that about?"

"Calm down. Whatever anger you feel toward her, I don't deserve to shoulder. You can leave if you plan to talk to me like that."

His face falls, and the wrath that was just evident disappears. "I'm sorry. She just . . . infuriates me."

My initial thoughts go to her deserting him on his fall, and I immediately have the urge to ease his pain. That's quickly replaced by the memory of her claiming that his story isn't the truth. What am I supposed to believe?

"Are you hungry?" I ask, deciding to table my wayward thoughts. He needs to fully calm down before I go down that road of questioning.

"No. I grabbed something on the way back."

I head toward the barn, climbing the steps to the loft in search of a banana for now. Zeke's on my heels the entire time, but he doesn't say anything. I've never been one that's felt the need to fill the quiet with forced conversation. I enjoy silence. It's therapeutic. But right now? It's awkward.

Zeke makes himself comfortable on my bed, while I peel the too-ripe banana and take an unsatisfying bite.

"Tired?" I ask around a mouthful.

"Frustrated."

I chew, giving myself time to organize the chaos of questions fighting for the top spot in my mind. All of them need to be asked, but the order and way in which I tackle these subjects will make all the difference. I don't want Zeke to shut down and subsequently shut me out.

"Did you know the humans are Nephilim?"

Zeke sits up, staring blankly into my eyes.

My lips purse and eyes widen in a *well, did you know* expression.

"Leeanna tell you that?"

I nod, because I don't want to give him too much.

He groans. "I suspected as much."

"Why didn't you tell me?"

"I was trying to determine how much Blaine and the others knew about their descent. I've always suspected they knew more than they were letting on."

"Did the topic come up today?"

"No. I didn't tell them about us."

My eyes narrow and nose scrunches. "Why? Wasn't that the point? To give them all of the sordid details?"

"I was trying to buy us some time to consult with local witches to see what provisions we can have created to help the humans into their powers."

"Do you think it makes sense to go to the coven before we even know for sure which lineage they descended from? That will make a huge difference in how we bring out their individual gifts."

"Fair point. I'll round them up tomorrow and we'll tell them everything."

I lie back and curl into Zeke's side. "Still want me to try to conjure that storm?"

"Nah. Not now." A yawn escapes Zeke's lips. "I'm wiped out. Tomorrow will be better. Let's rest tonight."

I remain snuggled into Zeke, but my thoughts keep straying to his story about falling. At the end of the day, that matters less than how we need to move forward with the Nephilim, but I can't help but question why Leeanna would claim he's not telling me the truth. Why lie? After what I told him, his story seemed parallel. What could possibly be worse than staging a fall with another angel—the devil included under that umbrella term?

"Did you fall for the reasons you said?"

The question is out before I can think better of it. Zeke stiffens, and it makes me wonder why. Is he thrown by the shift in conversation, or is that a tell that he's not being entirely truthful?

"Why would you ask me that? Did you talk to Leeanna about that?"

I shouldn't lie—I'm questioning him about lies—and yet a voice in the back of my head, one that sounds a little too much like Leeanna for my liking, urges me not to divulge my entire conversation with Leeanna.

"No. I just . . . I'm having a hard time seeing someone as high and mighty as Leeanna in a different light. That's all."

He huffs. "Leeanna isn't the perfect servant she attempts to convince everyone she is."

"That I don't doubt."

She's threatened to end me despite God's will. Serious or not, that, in and of itself, is a slight on God. His word is the almighty word, and she knows better than to question it.

"Let's not talk about Lee tonight. I want to spend time with you."

I lean up and place a kiss on Zeke's cheek. "What do you want to do?"

"Make out? Get to third base? Normal stuff."

I smirk. "You'll be lucky to get to second base before I fall asleep."

"Is that so?" he asks, practically jumping up to straddle me. "I think I can convince you to stay awake."

"You can try." I bite my lip, eliciting a groan from Zeke.

His lips press against mine and we're soon lost to sensation and pleasure as his hands run down my chest. He lifts my shirt and bra so that my breasts are bare to him. As good as his hands feel on me, I can't help being distracted by all the things Leeanna said.

I'm not sure that I trust a word she says, but something niggles, and I can't put my finger on it. Maybe I've allowed her to get into my head too much. Zeke's given me zero reason to question him, and until he does, I'm going to push down my worries and focus on the impending war. It's coming. Of that, I'm sure.

DEVIL DEVIL

Couldn't sleep. Gone to talk to Blaine and the others to get them on the same page. xx-Z

That's what I woke to. A note, basically cutting me out of the conversation that yesterday he thought it was important for me to be a part of. Then there's that niggling feeling still present from yesterday, which isn't helping my ultra-confused state about Zeke's actions.

Instead of stewing all day, I pick up my cell—that I rarely use—and dial Zeke. After three rings, he answers.

"Morning."

"Why didn't you wake me?" The question sounds more whiny than accusing and I cringe at that truth.

"You were tired. I didn't want to wake you."

"If you were that concerned about getting Blaine the information and having a united front, I think waking me would've been fitting."

"The more I thought about it, the more it didn't make sense. They don't know you. They don't trust you."

I bristle at this. The war doesn't care who trusts me. It's coming, and if any of us want to survive, differences need to be cast aside. Zeke knows this, and coddling the Nephilim during such a crucial time doesn't even make sense. He's a warrior. A fighter. He doesn't have time for games or childish behavior, yet now, at the most pressing of times, he's inviting both.

My question is why?

"Do what you have to, Zeke, but you and I both know that their feelings don't matter to Hell's army. They need to suck it up and prepare. Liking me has no relevance."

"Blaine doesn't want to discuss his lineage with you around. He'll share which order his father is from, but not who is father is."

"So you've already had the conversation with his group?"

"No. I'm on my way there now."

He lied. Last night he told me he wasn't sure if they were aware. He said he was trying to gauge whether they knew. If he hasn't gotten there yet, then by his own account of what he knows, they haven't talked about lineage or even confirmed that they are in fact Nephilim.

That niggling feeling morphs into suspicion and doubt. It brings life to Leeanna's words and has me rethinking my earlier stance. Perhaps I shouldn't write her off.

I dress quickly, needing to get out of this loft. The walls feel like they're closing in on me as the uncertainty mounts. A run is necessary to expel this negative energy, and a storm is vital.

My arms pump hard, propelling me forward down an overgrown path. I leap over roots and downed tree branches, never once halting my pace. Sweat beads and runs down my face, but I don't care. I like the proof of my efforts. When the last of my stored energy is depleted, I go in search of an open area, where I can summon my needed storm.

I'm in the middle of an open field, arms raised to the sky, preparing to begin my process, when the air around me shifts. Everything stills and the hairs on my neck stand on end. I'm in trouble.

"Victoria."

That voice.

It crawls over my skin like a million tiny spiders, but it isn't unpleasant, and that makes me instantly nauseous. Did my thoughts the other day conjure him? Because he's here and there is no doubt he's come to collect sooner than I expected. I am not prepared to see him, so I remain with my back to him. Not the best position to be in, but I have to trust that after everything, he'd give me a fair fight.

"Lucifer," I grind out, pushing as much indignation into my voice as I can muster without giving myself away. My legs are wobbly, and my entire body is quaking inside.

"Lucifer?" he asks, sounding almost insulted.

I feel him closing in on me until his chest is inches from my back. He doesn't touch me, yet every fiber of my being tingles, electrified. I can feel his warm breath tickle at the base of my neck. Perfidious goose bumps form all over.

"What? No more Luke?" he whispers into my ear.

My eyes slam shut at the onslaught of sensations his nearness causes. My body tenses and my hands ball into fists as I attempt to keep the emotions at bay.

"What do you want?" I murmur back, keeping my eyes closed, praying for this moment to end.

"He's not listening, love. He never does," he says, proving he's entered my mind.

"Get out of my head," I grate through clenched teeth.

He spins me around so that we're face to face, our lips so close that if I leaned in only a fraction, they'd touch.

It wouldn't be the first time.

My eyes meet his intense gaze.

"I didn't send those demons after you."

Such an odd conversation starter. Of all the things left unsaid between us, that's not where I thought this would begin.

"Why should I believe a word you say?"

"You have to know I'd never let anything happen to you. *I* saved you from the demons, zombies, and those pathetic excuses for angels," he seethes. His eyes search mine, looking for something I refuse to give him. "I've never stopped thinking about you, Victoria."

"Stop saying my name," I yell, feeling out of control and vulnerable for the first time in two years. "You're evil. You're vile," I say, clutching my head.

"You chose to fall. You did that all on your own," he says, sounding wounded, but I'm no fool. He's the king of deceit. I won't fall for it this time.

"You *lied* to me," I sneer. "You tricked me."

He pulls me closer to him, our chests touching, and the heat that runs through me is so intense I almost buckle under the weight of it. It's pleasure manifested, and I hate that he can make me feel this way. I hate that after everything, I still want to be in his arms.

It's his demonic power over me. Nothing more.

"I'm the only one who can make you feel whole," he says, and I don't react to the fact he's still in my head. "That fallen angel you've decided to shack up with can't make you feel the way I can. Do you think I don't know what you're doing?" he fumes. "If he were here now, I'd tear him limb from limb. I wouldn't end his life slowly. Not after what he's done."

"He didn't do anything. You're here because he has something you don't want him to have."

He nods. "True. I suppose you know me too well."

"I don't know you at all."

"Let's not lie to each other. I know you and your body—well, most of it—very well."

"You're disgusting." My teeth grind together and my hands ball into fists at my side.

"No, love. Territorial."

I bark a deranged laugh. "You don't own me, Satan. I'm with Zeke now. Deal with it."

"Where did he run off to?" Luke says, a knowing smirk plastered on his face. "Did he tell you about his little hookup with the Nephilim?"

"What do you know about the Nephilim?" There's only

one girl in the group I've met, and it was pretty obvious at our first meeting she didn't like me on the spot. I try to rein in the sudden surge of jealousy, because it doesn't matter. Luke's knowledge about what Zeke might be hiding is more important.

"We aren't skipping the gritty details of your boy's line of love affairs. It's too good to not discuss."

"You know what? It doesn't matter. I pushed him away for too long. What he did during that time isn't my business."

"Tell yourself that, love. I can practically taste your jealousy."

"I'm not jealous. It's me he sleeps beside."

Luke chuckles. "Then you won't be at all mad that he's known from the beginning who she is and what she is. Along with her band of Nephilim."

My blood boils. "How do you know this?"

"I know a great deal, Victoria. Stick around. I'll blow your mind with all my knowledge."

"Leave," I command, turning my back on him and preparing to summon the storm so I can take out my rage on the demons of New Orleans.

He huffs, "Calm down. He's not with her. He has some unfinished business with a certain archangel."

He's not in my head for once, which is obvious by how badly he's read me. It's knowing that he's been lying to me about the Nephilim, and for much longer than twenty-four hours, that bothers me. And that he lied to me about where he was headed.

"How do you know he's meeting Leeanna?"

"I had a minion follow him. Apparently, the angel is not very happy with him."

"Stop following Zeke." I'm not sure why I'm defending my current Judas, but I don't like Luke poking around my business, and Zeke and his lies are definitely my business.

"He's not good enough for you."

"And you are?" I yell, sounding more unhinged by the second.

"I can make you feel better than anyone on Earth, Victoria."

"You have an unfair advantage, Satan," I snap back, feeling more out of control every second I'm this close to him. "Given you're prince of lust and lies, I'd say it's all smoke and mirrors. Nothing about our time together was real."

"I've never lied to you. It was the truth you couldn't handle."

"You mean the truth about you being the devil," I screech, wanting to run away—anywhere to be far from him.

"It doesn't change that everything I said to you was fact. I'd have done anything to have you by my side, Victoria. You could've ruled with me."

"Stop," I say, clutching my ears to drown out his lies. "Just leave me alone."

"Look at me," he says, grabbing my hip with one hand and my chin with the other, forcing me to meet his incensed stare.

I glare, hoping that every single ounce of hate I bear for him seeps from my eyes and burrows deep into his blackened soul. Assuming he even has one.

He swallows and I watch as his Adam's apple bobs. Against every molecule of my being, my insides melt at the simple motion. Every word he's spoken makes me quiver with want. My body screams for me to give in to him, and I hate it. I tear my eyes away, wanting to punish myself for being so easily manipulated.

"You got what you wanted. I fell, Luke." His nickname slips too easily from my lips, and his eyes close, something serene passing over his face, making me loathe him even more. He doesn't get to relish in my weakness. "What else do you want to take from me?"

"I don't want to take anything, Victoria. I simply want

what I once had," he says, green eyes penetrating my every defense.

"What?" I say, sounding more tired than anything else.

"You."

I let out a bitter laugh. This dance between us is exhausting and demeaning. The fact that one profession of possession has a sense of peace falling over me proves that I've learned nothing. I'm a glutton for the devil's deceptions. I yearn for them. I might as well throw myself at his feet, offering my body as his concubine. I've fallen so far from grace.

"Go," I whisper, internally begging him to show me kindness this once.

He flinches, taking a step away from me, leaving me feeling colder than I have in a long time. I feel his loss so deeply, I almost beg him to hold me again.

"I'll go, Victoria. But this isn't the end. You owe me a debt." He disappears without another word.

Nothing has changed. I'm pathetic. He still holds my heart in his hands, and that truth alone makes me sick. I wish he'd end this cruel captivation and crush the worthless organ once and for all. I've been an empty shell for two years. Putting me out of my misery would be a kindness. Another one he owes me.

FIRST

Right after Luke did yet another disappearing act, the storm I'd been working on finally gave, reenergizing me. I did an hour HIIT workout, cleaned the loft, took a shower, paced the floor, and finally gave in and called Zeke. His voicemail picked up and I didn't leave a message.

I've avoided calling out of sheer guilt—a new emotion for me. I don't owe anything to Zeke, especially given his secrets, but I do feel guilty in general for the way I acted when Luke appeared. I didn't conjure him, but I didn't push him away either. A part of me wants to continue to lash out and blame Luke for my actions, but he didn't do it. I felt no magically engineered pull. He didn't cause me to act like I did. That was all me, and I'm ashamed. I all but humped his damn leg, the need for his touch so strong.

I'm ashamed because after everything, I still haven't learned my lesson.

Everything is different with Luke. When I'm around him, he sucks the air from my lungs, while simultaneously serving as my oxygen. The strong emotions have been there with Zeke too. Butterflies, tingles, all of it. The pull I feel to each of them is night and day.

Where Zeke's my calm, Luke's my storm. Zeke soothes,

while Luke's pull threatens to undo me. One is safe and the other puts me in free fall. At least, there had been a sense of security with Zeke, up until Leeanna forced me to examine Zeke without the rose-colored glasses. I didn't question my feelings for him, because I believed they were genuine. With Luke, I second-guess everything. Is he manipulating me? I question it because he has the ability to do such things. Now, both of them have me second-guessing myself.

My head and heart are at war as I battle my yo-yo thoughts.

"Ugh," I yell, and the force of it echoes off the walls.

My phone rings and I jump toward it. Zeke's name lights up the screen, and I can't answer it fast enough.

"Where are you?" I say, forgoing a simple hello. He doesn't deserve it right now.

"Hey, gorgeous. I'm on my way to Savannah."

"Savannah?" I bark. "Georgia? Why?"

"One of the hunters you met at the death house got a tip. Apparently, there's a coven in Georgia that knows what's happening and I'm going down with Chad to shake them down."

"You mean Nephilim," I correct harshly.

"Yeah, well, you know. Old habits."

"That was a really fast talk you had, if you and Chad are on your way to Georgia. I thought you were headed to Blaine?"

"Maeve intercepted me before I had time. She said I had to act fast."

"Maeve? The redhead?" I shriek, wanting to come through the phone and single-handedly beat Zeke senseless.

"That's the one," he says hesitantly. "But she's not coming along. I'm meeting back up with her when I get back."

"Great," I manage to muster through my haze of rage.

"To debrief with the whole group, Tor. Please trust me."

Trust.

It's funny how such absolute truths can be crushed in one

instant. I trusted Zeke with my life, and he literally stomped on that trust and doesn't even realize I know.

"Where were you before?" I sound like one of those insecure girlfriends who is always waiting for the other shoe to drop, and I hate it. That's not what this is. This is calling him—well, trying to—on his shit.

He groans. "Running errands." Lies. "This is the first chance I've had to call you."

My stomach rolls, knowing that he's leaving out the part about seeing Leeanna. The secrets keep adding up. All of the insecurities I'm feeling boil over, and tears well in my eyes. These damn human emotions are for the birds. I wipe the tears away roughly and decide to call him on it.

"Are you sure you weren't with Lee?"

"Baby, stop. What's this all about?"

Now he's diverting.

"Were you with her?" I press, needing him to come clean. Withholding this key piece means he's not to be trusted, and that will break me.

The line is quiet for a second, only managing to stress me out further. "Yes. But only because she asked me to meet her to discuss the humans—Nephilim."

"What about them?" I cluck my tongue and wait for him to explain.

"She stressed that they could only know so much. It was a warning."

"Why didn't you tell me that to begin with?"

He sighs. "I know she's a sore spot right now. I didn't want to leave with us on bad terms."

"You lied to me. I know you're hiding things, Zeke."

"Please don't do this. You know you're the only one I want."

These new emotions are too overwhelming. They're creeping in on all sides, and I'm about to burst. "It's not about that. Don't you get that I know you've known about the

128

Nephilim this whole time? I know you lied to me and you just keep lying, Zeke."

Putting myself out there like this is making me feel vulnerable. My heart is pounding and my stomach is flopping. Caring for someone is the worst in moments of uncertainty. Will he own his mistakes and offer understandable and forgivable reasons? Or will he continue to bury what could've been between us under his mountain of deceit?

His harsh sigh gives me hope that he realizes it's time to own it. "You're right. I've known for a long time. I didn't say anything because I couldn't. Leeanna and Michael told me. They said if I helped get the army of Nephilim trained and ready to fight, they'd consider allowing me—us—back in after the war."

I gasp at this revelation. "W-what? They did?"

"Don't get your hopes up, Tori. We have a long road ahead of us." He takes a deep breath. "I'll tell you everything when I get back. But right now, I need to focus on the task ahead. When Maeve got the call, it was stressed that time was of the essence. The coven is planning on going into hiding. I'm sorry, baby. I can't have this conversation right now."

My chest deflates and a random tear drips down my cheek. Those teen girls on TV have nothing over my weak ass. I cringe at the truth in that. Elation and irritation war for prominence in my jumble of emotions. I don't want to wait to have this talk. I'm desperate to know everything about this deal with Leeanna and Michael. Could there really be a chance of going home?

"I promise. We'll talk as soon as I get back."

"Fine," I concede. "Zeke, be careful. Call me when you know something."

I don't want anything to happen to Zeke, no matter what's going down. I can't do this alone, and despite the current situation, I care about him.

"Promise. Get some rest, Tori. I'll be home soon."

Home.

Everything is changing. He's calling me baby and referring to my loft as home, but considering there are still major secrets between us, none of it feels right anymore.

We're nowhere close to having our shit figured out. A future with Zeke sounds like a fantasy concocted in some romance novel I'd never read. Now that there's talk of getting back to Heaven, the idea seems ridiculous. Why start something that has no happily-ever-after for us? Would I even still want that if it was possible?

I'm angry, and a lot needs to be worked out. There's no sense in torturing myself until Zeke gets back. I need to get out of here for a bit. Zeke isn't the only one who can dig for answers. I have my own connections to local covens, and chances are, answers are closer to home than Zeke realizes.

Before I go chasing leads, I need to get my shit in order, and I need to live a little for me if my time here could come to an end soon. I suit up, knowing full well that once the sun sets and the moon is overhead, I'll be hunting. Perhaps before sunset, if the other day was any indication. Zeke would not be pleased, but he's not here. Solis at my back, I throw a black leather jacket over my shoulders to try to conceal the lethal weapon.

Tonight, I'm going to enjoy all aspects of the city, and then I'm going hunting for demons and answers.

I toured New Orleans like any other human new to the area would. The city's different in the light of day. It gives off a false sense of security, considering what's been roaming the area lately. Regardless of the evil that lurks, the city is alive and thriving.

My tour ends at Café Beignet on Bourbon Street. I'm seated outside, enjoying the music provided by a local jazz artist, when a small child lively dancing to the music catches my eye. Children have never been a source of entertainment for me. In truth, they annoy the hell out of me on a good day. This particular little girl, with her chestnut ringlets and bright brown eyes, has me captivated.

The longer she dances, the farther away she strays from her mother's side, and the woman doesn't even realize it. My eyes dart around to see if anyone else is paying attention, and when they land back on the girl, she's just disappearing out of sight around the corner. When her mother doesn't move to go after her, I spring to action. Why? God only knows.

She's got a good head start on me, and based on the size of the crowd loitering in the area, I have to appear human, which means she's getting farther ahead of me than I'm comfortable with. My head is screaming at me to not make this my business, but I can't do that. This city is magical, but it's also dangerous. I can't knowingly allow a child to venture away from her parent.

Why didn't I just alert her mother? It would've been the smart thing to do. Alas, here I am meandering through throngs of people, chasing after a girl I've never seen before in my life and have absolutely no connection to. She rounds corner after corner, steering us farther away from the crowds and into darker, even more dangerous areas of Bourbon Street.

When the last pedestrian is out of sight, I pick up my speed and run after her. We're on a back street. Every streetlamp's bulb has been burned out or busted out, leaving us in darkness. The only light I have is from the moon overhead. There's not a person around, and not a single light shines in any of the windows of the surrounding buildings.

The girl is sitting with her back turned to me in the middle of the street. I approach slowly, not wanting to alert her to my presence, for fear she'll take off and the chase will start all over. The closer I get, the more I choke on dread. Something isn't right.

The instant I have that thought, a high-pitched cackling sounds surrounds me. The screeching comes from every side, yet it's still just me and the girl. My head turns back to the spot in the road, but the girl is gone. In her place is a box sitting innocently, but its mere presence indicates it's anything but.

I make my way to that spot in the street, bending to pick up the box while my head swivels to keep an eye on my surroundings. It's a plain wooden box with no etchings or decorative painting. My instincts tell me to put it down and vacate the area, but when have I ever run from a potential fight?

My right hand goes to my back, patting Solis to affirm I'm not alone in what's to come. Without overthinking it any longer, I pop the top of the box and stare down to find a bloody, beating heart.

I drop the offending object and take a colossal step away from it. What. The. Hell.

"I see you got my gift." An unfamiliar voice sounds from behind me, and I spin around to come face to face with a creature that's undoubtedly an upper-echelon demon.

At first glance he appears human. Chiseled cheekbones, raven hair, devastating smile—it's all there. But I know what to look for. That shimmery glamour just at the edges gives him away. If I focus for just a few seconds on that shimmer, it'll start to fade away and the demon's true identity will be revealed. This particular demon is strong. After several seconds of trying to uncover the glamour, I'm only able to capture glimpses.

"Who are you?" I ask, grabbing for Solis.

The demon tsks. "Is that any way to repay me? I think a thank you is in order."

I do the most unladylike thing I can think of and spit at his feet. "There's your thank you, demon."

"I'm going to enjoy enslaving you," he sneers. "I see why Lucifer is so taken with you. You truly are a rare beauty."

Definitely top rank, if he knows my past with Lucifer.

"Good luck. You have no idea how much trouble you're in. Coming for me alone? Big mistake."

He chortles. "You think I came alone? Oh, no. I brought friends."

He whistles, and the shadows all around me start to form into creatures that get uglier as they materialize.

He brought a horde, and that isn't good for me.

HELP

I'M COMPLETELY SURROUNDED. Solis is with me and I'm powered up, but even I would have a hard time taking on this many demons. Demons who are at the mercy of one of Satan's chief demons.

"Lucifer," I scream, hoping he'll come to my aid again.

"He can't hear you, but feel free to scream all you want." His eyes darken until they're completely black. "I live off the fear. Run, little angel. The chase is my favorite part."

His wicked sneer would typically garner one of my own. Egotistical demons are usually the easiest to take down, but I know that this time, that won't be the case. This situation isn't impossible, but it's going to test my strength more than it's been tested since falling.

Demons are notorious liars, so I disregard his warning and yell out for Lucifer again.

"Like I said, he can't hear you." He taps on a gaudy oval sapphire hanging around his neck.

"Witches."

"Very powerful witches."

"They'll eventually turn on you. Witches have their own agenda. Always."

He taps his chin like he's contemplating my words, but

soon, a Cheshire-cat grin spreads across his wickedly handsome glamoured face. "You aren't wrong. It's the coven leader's heart in that box. I figured you'd like to eat the heart of the witch that single-handedly doomed Earth."

I cringe. "Pass. But thank you."

"Such manners," he says, walking closer.

His hand shoots forward, and I crouch, but his action only causes the box to lift into the air and fly into his outstretched arms.

"We're not going to waste a perfectly good heart."

He puts the bloody organ to his mouth and inhales deeply before taking a bite out of it. I turn my head away in disgust.

"Between the power that Lucifer bestowed upon me and this charm, even Lucy himself won't hear your call before you're in my control." I turn my head back to the demon.

"What do you want with me?"

"You'll be one of my first—and favorite—trophies."

"Since when do demons take angels as trophies?" I ask with a raised brow.

"Never. We don't allow them to live."

I throw my head back and laugh, because in all the wars of history between Heaven and Hell, there have been far more casualties of Hell than Heaven.

"You're the exception because you're *his* angel. I'll take his love and then his throne."

I stop laughing, because there is so much wrong with that declaration. Starting with the obvious—there's no love between Lucifer and me. Hate? Yes. Love? Hell no.

Liar.

"Get her, boys. But remember, not a hair is to be taken from her head."

With that, they all crowd in around me. I'm in my fighting stance with Solis at the ready. The first demon steps forward, and it's clear he's already injured, by the way he drags his leg behind his body. They're throwing their weakest links at me first to try to wear me out. Not a bad plan.

With one solid swing, his head is detached from his shoulders, and his body disintegrates before it even hits the ground.

"Who's next?" I say, lifting my fingers in a *come get it* gesture.

This time the entire line of demons in front of me moves forward. I haven't so much as broken a sweat, but the task ahead has me wishing it were already over.

The line stops suddenly, eyes lifted to the sky. That's when I hear them. Angel wings flapping in the air, feathers rustling. I didn't realize how much I missed that sound until now.

"What do we have here?" Leeanna says from my side. "Finally, you showed yourself. Foolish demon," she sneers.

I watch the thing closely. He doesn't so much as flinch. No fear, which is something different. He really is arrogant.

In the blink of an eye, he disappears, and demons melt back into the shadows.

Coward after all. Or simply smarter than most, which doesn't bode well. A stupid demon is much easier to send back to Hell.

"He's got bigger plans. No way was he going to waste even a portion of his army on this fight," Leeanna muses. "Glad to see they didn't have time to tear you limb from limb."

"I didn't think you cared what happened to me."

"We need you for the war. After? I couldn't care less." She says it, but the way her chin quivers gives away the lie. Despite my fall, Leeanna does care.

"What's going to happen when I get back into Heaven? You'll have to drop this better-than-thou act."

Her eyes narrow. "You've got a long way to go before that's even a blip of a possibility."

I shrug. "We'll see."

"What was that thing around his neck?" Michael cuts in, drawing both Leeanna's attention and mine.

"A witch's medallion. He ate the heart of the witch who gifted it to him."

Leeanna grimaces. "That only made him more powerful."

"He's able to create some type of barrier to shield himself and the surrounding area."

I leave off the part where I called out to Lucifer and he never came.

"Most barrier spells with a medallion last only a short time."

Would've been great to know that minutes ago. Then again, the angels hearing me call out for help from the devil wouldn't bode well for me.

"We know you have connections to covens in the area," Leeanna grinds out. "We need you to find out what they know that could be helpful to us."

"You want me to consort with witches?"

Michael's head snaps to hers and she nods, but her eyes are cast down, knowing what she's asking is wrong.

"In this instance, if they have information we need, we have to."

"Leeanna, you can't ask that of her."

"She's fallen, Michael. Who else can go to them?"

He purses his lips but appears to come to the same conclusion she did. I'm their only chance of working with the witches.

"Fine, but if I do this, you both have to promise you'll speak on my behalf if and when the time comes for me to stand trial to get back into Heaven."

"If that happens," Michael hisses, "I'll speak for you. Assuming you toe the line in every other aspect. Work against us, and you'll get nothing from me."

It's my turn to nod.

I step up to Leeanna. "Why did you meet with Zeke earlier?"

She stiffens. "H-how do you know about that?"

I internally cringe, as my source would not go over well for me.

"He let it slip," I lie. "But he wouldn't tell me what you talked about."

137

She puffs out her cheeks. "Zeke didn't fall for me. He didn't fall at all. He's here to make sure you stay and fulfill your punishment here on Earth."

"What?" I jerk back. "What does that even mean?"

"Isn't it obvious?" Michael jeers. "He's been working against you all along."

My body sways and my eyes glaze over.

They have to be lying. He wouldn't. Couldn't.

"He did, Victoria." Leeanna's tone isn't mocking. It's sympathetic, and I might hate that more. "He's here on assignment."

"I-I'm the assignment?"

She simply nods.

The son of a bitch tricked me. He took my virginity, and straight up lied to me. He's no better than Lucifer, and he will feel my wrath.

HELL FROZE OVER

THE NEXT MORNING, I'm strolling the far end of Bourbon Street. On this side of town, every vice a sinner has can be sated. Sex permeates the air even at this time of day. Behind any of these walls, I'd likely find myself in the middle of an orgy, complete with drugs and alcohol flowing like a waterfall —never ending.

My mind is numb as I focus on the task at hand, using all the energy I have left to smash out the human emotions that are trying to break through. I'm done feeling.

I look at the peeling numbers above the shops as I pass, but in the end, there's no need. The place I'm looking for stands out from every other building. The Solheim Coven doesn't have to go for inconspicuous. While every other building on either side of this block is dilapidated, the home of one of the most highly respected voodoo priestesses in the South is well kept, with a fresh coat of paint. However, only magical beings can see it. The home has been shaded so that to everyone else, it looks like every other building—well on its way to collapsing.

The blood-red front door stands out starkly against the bright white on every other surface. A black wrought-iron fence surrounds the home, likely to keep the drunken partygoers who stray too far from the heavily lit part of Bourbon Street off its pristine lawn.

Magic swirls in the air, so thick I can taste it. It coats every surface, leaving a shimmering gleam that only a magical being can see. This signals that the woman I came to see is here: Madame Solheim, the oldest sister of the Solheim Coven. I knock briskly four times before turning the knob and allowing myself in. I know the drill; I've been here before, but never in the daytime.

The foyer of the house is quiet, and there's not a person in sight. I walk toward the back, make a right down the long narrow hallway, and pass through the curtain of beads hanging in the doorway to the heart of the place. The coven sits in a circle, holding hands and chanting, while sage burns in the center.

I don't dare interrupt whatever they are doing. It would be considered a slight against the coven, and I'm not here to incur their wrath. I need their help, and I'll only get it by being patient.

Several minutes go by with the same chant being crooned. My arms are crossed over my chest and I have to try extra hard to not roll my eyes.

"Still wearing that chip firmly on your shoulder, angel?"

When had the chanting stopped?

I clear my throat, but she silences me with a raised hand.

"Leave us," she says to her sisters, and they stand, exiting the room without a single glance in my direction.

Madame Solheim stands and makes her way to me. "There's evil in the air. We're trying to purify as much as we can," she explains the act that I just witnessed.

"You know why I'm here," I say, with a bit of reverence for her gift. I should've come straight here before tracking down Almada. I would've saved myself time.

"Nah. Almada had your answers." My eyes narrow in on the mind reader.

This woman goes against everything I was taught. She

embodies the very essence of heretics. What she practices goes against God's law and will be punishable by eternal damnation.

She sighs. "Still holding on to those archaic beliefs?"

"No, I was merely reflecting on a time where I would've only stepped foot in here to end your life and send you to Hell," I admit.

Madame Solheim appreciates frank discussion, and today is no different. She smiles, nodding her head. "Sometimes falling isn't a bad thing, Tori. You have the ability to see different views for what they are . . . simply different. We can all live peacefully."

"You believe that?"

"Someday, but not today," she confesses. "Something wicked this way comes."

"He's already here."

She shakes her head, holding up one finger. "Not him."

"Who's more wicked than the devil himself?"

I ask the question more for confirmation. After what I witnessed last night, I know exactly who's after the throne of Hell.

"Something that wishes to harness the powers of Hell to unleash it onto the world. Something that wishes to defy *him*."

"So, it is a coup," I say aloud.

"Mmm," she murmurs. "But you already knew that."

"Who is it? I might've faced him, but I never heard his name."

She tsks. "You give me too much credit, daughter of God."

"I'm no daughter of God. In fact, he'd probably smite you just for saying so."

She laughs. "I was smitten long ago. I don't fear God."

She should. God is not to be underestimated. He could end Earth and Hell in one tantrum, if he so chose. His love for all mankind knows no bounds; otherwise, this earth would've been scorched long ago. He too has faith. Faith in the faithless.

His belief in humans is unearned and unrequited in many ways.

"So, you don't know what we're up against?"

"Pure evil. If Lucifer doesn't act, it'll be too late."

"You want Lucifer to succeed? Why?" I'm truly mystified by this entire conversation.

"Not everything is black and white, Victoria. There are things that not even you know about the inner workings of Heaven and Hell."

"And you do?"

She shrugs. "I've heard whispers."

"Care to share?"

"Some things are not for me to tell. This is a conversation you'll have, and soon. But not with me."

My lips form a thin line as I debate whether to take my chances and push or move on, knowing full well that Madame Solheim only shares what she wishes. I inhale and blow the air out hard.

"Who is the coven helping the demon?"

"A wicked lot."

"Where can I find them?" I press, ready to start hunting witches along with demons.

"They've already moved underground. Ezekiel was too late. Whoever the creature, it's protecting them for their service. Not even my coven can uncover their whereabouts."

"Is Zeke in danger?" I don't want anything to happen to him until he feels every ounce of the pain I'm going to inflict on him for his damn deceit.

She shakes her head. "He'll be fine. He needs to worry about you more than anything."

"Does he have any idea I know he betrayed me?" The words are spoken from between my teeth as anger takes hold.

"No."

"I'm going to find him and tear him limb from limb."

"No. Forget about Zeke. You need to go to Lucifer. He's very worried about you. I can feel his distress."

My nose scrunches. "Lucifer doesn't care about me. I'm just another toy."

"You know better than that, Victoria. You're nothing close to a toy for him."

I refuse to even dissect those words. Even Solheim can be wrong.

"This creature is determined to reign over Hell. Lucifer needs to be ready. The entire world depends on him sitting upon that throne."

It's worse than I feared. A rogue demon, creating an army to overthrow Lucifer. It's a sad day when the devil isn't even evil enough. He kept his demons in line, and one stepped off the path. Whoever is threatening his reign clearly has other ideas in mind, and it does not bode well for mortals.

"Thank you, Madame Solheim," I say, turning to go.

"Victoria," she calls, and I look back at her over my shoulder. "We all deserve to be heard."

I furrow my brows at her cryptic message, and she continues.

"Not all that are fallen are truly bad, and not all that reign are entirely virtuous."

"You're talking in riddles."

"Hear him out, Victoria. There is much to learn from the man who stole your heart and haunts your dreams." With that, she walks past me and disappears.

Maybe if Hell froze over. Perhaps her witchy signal is getting Zeke and Lucifer confused.

I'm still contemplating her words on my stroll down Bourbon Street. As if the world weren't already filled to the brim with evil, something worse threatens to take over. For as much as I resent my time on Earth, I'm beginning to fear it'll be cut too short. I hardly allow myself time to enjoy any part of it.

The sun is dipping down behind the landscape, painting the sky in brilliant shades of orange and pink. I marvel at the beauty of God's Earth.

As a virtue angel, I never truly understood his fascination with his creation. I always thought humans were powerless weaklings that held no appeal and Earth was simply their dwelling. Now that I'm here and have time to open my eyes and look around, I get it. It's a true masterpiece. As hurt as I was at being cast out and losing my wings, I can't help but feel a bit lucky. It's something I don't deserve, but getting to experience this place and all the intense emotions that come with it feels like an unspoken gift.

With war on the horizon and the possibility of the end close by, I vow here and now to look up to the sky a bit more, inhale the scents of flowers that waft in the air, and enjoy all the trappings of Earth while I can.

Take Madame Solheim's advice to heart and allow others their voice.

I'm not in the market to have conversations with the devil about anything other than saving the world, but it looks like that's exactly the talk we need to have. If I have information that could be helpful to keep him in power and the balance in order, then I'll give it to him. The only problem? How does one summon the devil and not alert the other enemy?

BLAME

My tires squeal as I turn the corner a little too hard. After meeting with Madame Solheim and having my moment of reflection, I know what needs to be done. I rushed back to my loft and dusted off the old Ford pickup that's been rusting away under a sheet in the barn.

Having spent my existence as an angel who flew everywhere, learning to drive hasn't come naturally, and for the sake of the other drivers on the road, I typically choose to walk—or run—everywhere. Unfortunately for any unsuspecting human in my path tonight, neither walking nor running is an option now. I have to go too far, so the trusty black beast gets to put its wheels to the pavement.

I've been driving for an hour when finally, a mile up the road, I see the entrance to St. Joseph Cemetery. The fact that I've spent entirely too much time in cemeteries as of late isn't lost on me.

The iron gates are open as if expecting my visit. Typically, they're closed at sundown, and I expected to need to break in. At least one thing has gone my way tonight. I pull in and drive to the very back, out of view from the road. The truck rolls to a stop and I cut the engine, jumping out and shutting the door as quietly as possible. The cemetery is in the middle of the country, away from prying eyes, but I still don't want to attract any unwanted attention, including that of the spirits who roam the cemetery.

There's a chill in the air, and a light blanket of mist hovers over the expanse of the grounds. The mostly full moon overhead shines down, giving the area just enough light to cast shadows between the tombs. On a typical night, St. Joseph's would be creepy, but tonight, there's a foreboding energy twirling through this place, causing goose bumps to pebble over my arms.

These grounds have acted as the setting to a demon bloodbath once before. It's the very place I was first called by Luke. Tonight, the tables are turning and I'm summoning him.

"Lucifer," I call out, arms spread above my head as if I were worshipping on a Sunday morning at church. "I know you hear me," I accuse, not really knowing if it's true, but hoping like hell it's that easy. "I need you," I say, trying to not squirm at the blasphemy.

"I never thought I'd hear those words out of your mouth," Luke says from behind me, and the intense relief that he of all people came almost makes me sick, but this one time I actually do need him.

"You and me both," I quip, turning toward him.

Seeing him has the same effect it always does. It's the equivalent of my breath rushing out of my body on an exhale. Falling from the sky, wings splayed out as I glide to earth, ready for battle. Equal parts exhilaration and liberation. Completely concerning and something I need to work to suppress.

The reminder of my thorough lack of self-control changes the mood from civil to hostile in one second flat, and Luke doesn't miss the shift.

"Still blaming me for all your issues, love?"

My face burns in outrage. "Because it *is* your fault."

"Do I have to remind you of that little thing called free will?"

"I'm not a human." I bite the words. "You and I both know that even here, I'm nothing more than a pawn. If I act out of place, God won't hesitate to end me now. There's no predestined fate to protect me."

He puts his hands up, shrugging in his arrogant *maybe so, but it doesn't change the facts* way. "I never forced your feelings."

I choke out a humorless laugh. "Say what you want, but you were controlling our every interaction when you conned me into falling for you."

The cocky smile drops from his face. "I might have the ability to bend you to my will, love, but I never would. When you fell, that was your choice. I never forced your hand."

I take a threatening step toward him, finger raised in anger. "You pretended to care. You fooled me into thinking you were my soul mate."

My hand drops to my side and my head snaps away from his intense gaze. Admitting that's how I felt—to him, of all people—is humiliating. If I felt like a fool then, I feel even worse now.

"I *never* pretended to care, Victoria. I meant everything I said. All of it."

"Stop," I whisper, turning my back to him. "Everything bad that's happened is your fault."

His heavy breath is at my back, and I stiffen at his proximity. "If pinning this all on me helps you, then I'll gladly shoulder the burden."

I inhale deeply, trying to control my shaking body. I came here for reasons more important than rehashing our past. It would do no good to stay on this carousel of pointing fingers. A war is upon us, and in a twisted turn of events, I need to work with the devil. Just this once.

There are worse things than Lucifer ruling Hell, and the recent changes prove that theory.

"Thank you," he says, proving he's once again in my head.

"Ugh! See? Get out of my damn head."

I spin around, and he's mere inches from me. Taking a step back, I put some much-needed distance between us.

"You're distressed. I was trying to uncover the source." He's not playing around. His eyes are narrowed and his mouth is in a straight line, as though he's trying to rein in his temper. "What's wrong, Victoria?"

He senses my fear, and it throws me off kilter.

"How can you read me so well?" I say, hating the amazement in my voice.

"Like I said, you're radiating distress. I can practically taste it," he scoffs, but not at me, at my reaction. "Who's hurt you, Victoria? I swear I'll end them."

I lower my head. "Too many people lately."

"I'm going to murder Ezekiel."

My head snaps up at Luke's premature threat of violence. "Would you stop? I didn't come for your help in homicide. I'm here to warn *you*."

His lips curl into a wide smile that takes over his entire face. "Warn me? Why, love, you wound me if you think I require warning about anything."

"It's not funny, Luke. One of your demons has been laying the groundwork to overthrow you. He's working with a coven, and they've created rings that allow demons to come out in the daylight. He has a damn amulet around his neck to hide himself from you." My voice pitches and hands fly up into the air in exasperation, as this information does nothing to change his expression of carelessness.

He nods his head and begins to clap. "I must say, your detective work is sexy as hell, love. You could give the FBI a run for their money."

I groan, running my hands down my face in agitation. "Luke, stop. I'm serious. This is bad."

He moves toward me, placing his hands on my shoulders. I know he means to calm me—and he does—but he also manages to set my insides on fire. He has to realize how his touch affects me still. Even after everything, the pull to him is so strong, I want to fall to my knees and beg him not to leave me again. I shut my eyes tightly, trying to shake off the disgusting way he controls me without even trying.

"I know about the plan, and I can assure you he'll never win, Victoria. I've got it under control."

My breathing is ragged from the effort it's taking to keep my cool.

"A witch friend says otherwise. This coven the creature is working with is dark, Luke."

His eyes watch me closely. "Darker than me?"

Our heads are close, mere inches apart. If I leaned in, I could feel his lips on mine once more. "I . . ."

"Victoria." My name slips off his tongue, sounding like a virtue, and my eyes close, unwilling to allow him to see how affected I am.

"Please stop touching me," I say in a controlled voice, trying to show restraint. His hand falls from my shoulder, trailing a slow line down my arms, causing goose bumps to rise in their wake. The warmth disappears with the loss of his touch.

"I'm glad to see I'm not the only one affected by our proximity," he says, smiling boyishly, and I internally grimace at just how much it affects me. This is the Luke I fell for, charming and playful. Being here like this with him isn't good for me.

"I was almost killed, Lucifer. That doesn't seem like you have everything under control," I say wearily. "Unless you don't care about my life."

"That was an unfortunate slip that will never happen again." His words come out as a near growl, his fists are clenched at his sides, and his face contorts, showcasing a barely contained rage.

"He said he planned to capture me as a trophy."

Luke's features darken and I take a step back, frightened by the depth of darkness I see.

149

"He will never touch you again." The words are grated through his teeth.

"A war is brewing, Lucifer. I know it. The Nephilim know it. And so do the angels. You need to quit with the ego and admit it. You don't have this under control. Leeanna and Michael are so desperate they sent me to the coven."

His brows raise. "Bastards are scared. Good."

"We can't beat his army if we don't work together."

"Never. I'll do this alone."

I roll my eyes, tired of this conversation going in circles.

"Then I'll leave you to finish whatever game you're playing with your demons," I say, turning my back on him. "I suggest you end it soon. It's getting out of hand." I open the door to the truck and look over my shoulder once more at Luke. "If you ever cared for me at all, Lucifer, I beg you to end this."

I climb in and slam the door shut, turning the key, still in the ignition, but the damn thing won't start. "Damn it." I slam my fist into the steering wheel, hating that I couldn't even be allowed the satisfaction of an exit on my terms. My head falls back in frustration, hitting the back of the headrest. "Ouch," I call out, rubbing the back of my head.

"Need some help?" Luke asks, leaning into the open truck window, smirking at my misfortune. I want to wipe the damn smile from his lips.

"Do I really have to ask? Can you, for once, just do something nice?"

He pops an eyebrow. "Does that sound like me?"

"Ugh," I moan in irritation, and the bastard has the audacity to laugh. "I've killed for smaller infractions, Lucifer. If I were you, I'd be leery."

He smothers his smile with his fist. "You're right. I apologize. Let me get this working for you."

He starts to roll up his sleeves. "Pop the hood, would you?"

My nose crinkles in confusion. "Lucifer, what the hell are you doing?" I ask, getting out of the truck.

"Okayyy. Guess I'm on my own here," he says, tilting his head to the side and clenching his teeth, before lifting his hand and magically popping it open himself. "There," he muses. "Now let's see what's going on."

"Use your magic so I can get the hell out of here," I say, exasperated. "I have an hour-long drive home and I'm tired."

"I've never used my powers with you, and I'm not going to start now. We do this the mortal way."

"You just used your powers," I deadpan, motioning toward the opened hood.

He sighs. "That was an unfortunate slip. Won't happen again."

I'm still stuck on the whole *I've never used my powers with you* part. I'm sure that's a lie, but I'm struggling to conjure an instance to prove him wrong. He appears so sincere, and herein lies my problem. I'm easily duped by his charm. Or am I being too hard on him? A wise witch did tell me to hear him out, after all. Tonight, however, will not be that night. When I look back, he's still inspecting the guts of my dead truck.

"Oh my God, Luke, please."

"Using your creator's name in vain now, are you?"

"Don't start," I say, sounding worn out.

He eyes me curiously. "You aren't in any position to drive, angel."

I stiffen at that name. For so many reasons, I hate when he says it. It's like he's mocking me, and I instantly want to punch him.

"I'm sorry, *Victoria*." he amends. "Let me get you home. I'll make sure your truck gets back too."

"I don't want your help, Lucifer," I bite, and he frowns.

"You did a moment ago. Don't be too proud, love. I just want you to get home safe."

I sigh heavily, wanting to be in my bed, wrapped in my down comforter, away from this being that confuses me on so many levels. "Okay," I finally acquiesce.

"Okay." He smiles a closed-lip smile. "Close your eyes, and when you wake, you'll be back at your loft."

"Do you promise?" I level him with a raised brow and thinned lips.

"Where else would I send you?" His nose is scrunched, as if I just insulted him on the highest level.

"Just promise. No funny business."

He nods. "Home. To your feather bed. *Alone.*" He stresses the last word as though he has any control over who ends up in my bed.

I do as he instructs, and right before anything happens, I realize what he's just said.

The asshole knows where I live.

Of course he does.

EVERYBODY RISE

THE ALARM CLOCK on my nightstand blares some song about waking up with a curse, and I groan in response. The fact that the alarm was set in the first place annoys me, as I have nowhere to be. I reach over, grabbing the cord and yanking it from the wall. The music stops, leaving me in peaceful silence once again.

I kick the heavy down comforter to the end of the bed, too warm to be comfortable.

"I must say, love, I'm quite fond of that lacy thong. Black is definitely your color."

I jump up, squealing in horror at finding Luke in my room. On my bed.

"What the hell are you doing here?" I shriek.

Without looking fazed in the slightest, he jumps right in. "You owe me."

I clutch the covers to my half-naked chest. "Like hell I do."

He tsks. "Don't tell me you forgot how I saved you from Rix."

"Rix?" I ask, voice rising in confusion.

"My hound," he explains, picking a piece of lint off his black T-shirt.

He's dressed in head-to-toe black, and it takes everything in me not to drool. The T-shirt molds to his body like a second skin, showcasing his toned arms. He looks absolutely sinful, and at this moment, still half asleep, I admit I'd give just about anything for a taste.

A slow grin spreads across Luke's face. "That can absolutely be arranged."

"Ugh," I cry out, hating that he can read me so easily. "Get out." I point to the door.

"No can do. I came to collect, and I'm not leaving until your debt is settled."

"I didn't ask you to save me."

"You did. It was unspoken, but"—he taps his head—"I can read your mind and you wanted saving. And your debt keeps mounting."

"How so?"

"Last night I saved you from having to drive home in that death trap you call a truck."

"You are the most frustrating man I've ever met," I say through clenched teeth.

"I'm not a man, love. I'm so much more, and you know it."

"Semantics. You have the parts."

He smirks. "Yes, well in that regard, I guess you could say I'm all man. Care to see?" He waggles his brows and I roll my eyes.

"Pass," I quip, standing from the bed, not even trying to hide my basically bare ass.

Look, but you're never touching.

"Get on with it, Luke. What do you want?"

He clears his throat. "A date."

I turn back toward him. "A date? With whom?"

"I thought that was rather obvious," he says, tilting his head.

"Nope. No way," I say, shaking my head and turning

around to sift through my dresser. I'm so caught off guard, I don't even remember what I was looking for.

"Red cropped shirt," he says. "It's in the back." I have to take a deep breath so as not to react to his constant invasion of my inner thoughts.

"Think of something else for payment," I press forward, wanting to get this conversation over with, so that he'll leave me the hell alone.

"It's non-negotiable. That's what I want," he says, crossing his arms over his chest.

"It's never happening. Besides, I'm expecting Zeke back any moment, and I have a lot to say."

"He's not coming home."

My eyes narrow. "What exactly does that mean?"

"It means, you say yes. If you'd like him to return sometime this century, you'll pay up."

I spin on him. "Fine. Do what you must with him. You're saving him from my wrath."

"We need him for the war."

It's the first time Lucifer has admitted there will be a war. Even if it was in a roundabout way.

"Let me get this straight. You say we need him, but you're threatening him?"

"I'm simply saying he can run errands for the next decade, if that's what it takes."

I huff, crossing my arms over my chest. "I'll go wherever you want me to, but it's not a date, Luke. After it's done, you return Zeke. Unharmed."

"You have a lot of requirements for a debtor. Just agree and all will be right in your world again."

"What are the full terms? No tricks, Satan."

He chuckles. "Glad to see your rage is still intact. I was thinking you were going soft on me."

I wave my hands in the universal sign for *get on with it.*

"Twenty-four hours. We start with breakfast, hang out all

day, have dinner, stay out all night and sleep together. Your debt is paid at sunup."

My laugh comes out sounding maniacal. "You've lost your damn mind. I'm not sleeping with you. Twenty-four hours is astronomical."

"Your life isn't worth a simple twenty-four hours?"

"It's not worth giving my body to you," I say, covering my exposed midriff with the red shirt he knew I was searching for.

"I didn't say anything about sex, Victoria. I said sleep."

"Sleep together were your exact words and everyone knows the devil is in the details."

"Touché," he says, pursing his lips. "Then let me clarify," he stands, walking toward me and removing the shirt away from my stomach and discarding it on the bed behind him. "I only want to spend time with you. Nothing more. Nothing less."

"And if I don't? What really happens?"

"Rix will drag you to Hell."

His penetrating stare unnerves me and weakens my knees. "Promise me. No tricks."

"You have my word," he says, nodding curtly. "Now get dressed. We're going to breakfast," he calls out over his shoulder as he heads down the loft stairs, leaving me alone to ponder just what I've gotten myself into.

Fifteen minutes later, I'm dressed and descending the stairs. He's waiting at the bottom, looking up at me as though I'm his prom date unveiling my dress for the first time. His eyes are wide, and his mouth is agape.

I hide a smile under a contrived yawn. Something about the way he's looking at me has my walls dropping. He's making me feel important, which makes it even more imperative that I guard myself with him.

"Ready?" I ask, walking right past his outstretched hand.

When I make it outside, I stop in my tracks at the sleek black car that waits. "An Audi R8? What's the occasion?"

"Valentine's Day," he deadpans.

"It's April."

"So we're celebrating late. I thought you might like to ride in something that is sure to actually start and not rust out while we dine," he says, motioning to my truck.

"My truck runs."

"It didn't the other night."

He opens the passenger door for me, and I stop, turning toward him. "What are you up to?" I ask, searing him with a look of warning. *If you mess with me, I'll find a way to end you.*

"I'm just trying to have a semi-normal day. With you. Could you relax and try to enjoy yourself?"

"If I agree and truly try, do you swear to me that you'll leave me alone? No more drop-ins. We work together to end this evil and that's it. No more invading my dreams. One day and that's all?"

"You dream about me?" He smirks, and I groan. "Please, tell me what sordid things we do. I'll live vicariously through your nighttime imaginings."

My entire body feels like it's on fire from pure embarrassment. Why did I have to mention the damn dreams?

I don't say another word until we're seated on the patio of a café in the Garden District. Across the street is one of the oldest cemeteries in New Orleans, and as creepy as that should feel, considering I'm sitting with the devil at my side, it's actually quite beautiful in the light of day.

"What are you thinking?" Luke asks, examining the area.

I turn my gaze on him. "Nothing, really. I'm a fan of this part of town."

His eyes roam the area, seemingly unimpressed. "It's a bit boring for my taste, but I suppose it's a nice change of pace."

"Boring? Do you mean lacking debauchery?"

"A bit of debauchery never hurt anyone, love."

"Why do you call me *love*? What happened to *angel*?" I ask, rolling my eyes.

"For those of us in the underground, that carries derogatory connotations." He picks at something on his fingers, not meeting my eyes. "As you are no longer walking with the hordes of heavenly angels, I thought a changeup would suit."

"Let me get this straight. That whole time, what I thought was an endearment was really an insult?"

"Quite."

I huff. "You're evil."

He smirks. "Says who?"

"Everyone," I snap, growing annoyed with him.

"That's only because they've been fed the wrong narrative. The story you've heard is not the whole story."

I raise my eyebrow. "You want me to believe there's more to the story? That I shouldn't judge a book by its cover and all that."

He nods. "Exactly."

"If you're not evil, then what are you, Luke?" I lean forward, dying to hear how he's going to spin this one. The smirk on my face dies when I see how serious he is. His expression bounces from nervous to frustrated, and I'm not sure how to take this outwardly vulnerable side of him.

"I'm the caretaker of Hell. Just like inmates need wardens here on Earth, Hell does too."

"You incite sin, Luke. That's not what a warden does. They prevent evil deeds."

"That's what I do as well."

I shake my head. "Father cast you to Hell because you embodied evil."

He tsks, wagging his finger. "I challenged him, and he retaliated with a punishment, damning me to rule over the truly evil."

"What about the Bible and all the teachings?"

He scoffs. "That old thing? Do you not know this world's history? The early days of humanity were brutal. Order was nonexistent. The Bible is merely stories that God whispered into the ears of men, giving them something to hold over other humans, to keep them in line."

"How so?"

"Humans fear the unknown. They need something to explain what happens after this life. They need a reason to toe the line. Fear the devil and Hell, and you stay in line."

There is logic in his words, but why would God damn his son for simply questioning things? Lucifer was his favorite. He adored him. The punishment doesn't seem to fit the crime.

"He was trying to teach me a lesson, while also giving me the opportunity to experience life, which is all I wanted."

"You wanted to be human?"

"I wanted to feel something more than what was allowed in Heaven."

His gaze pierces mine, and there's a shift in the air. I don't speak and neither does he. Several minutes go by and I avoid his stare at all costs. When I finally do turn my head toward him, he seems more relaxed.

"Tell me something true," he says, leaning back in the flower-patterned yellow chair. I lick the inside of my lips, stalling. I don't want to talk. I'd rather sit here in peace, order food, and get the hell on with this sham of a day.

"Not happening, princess. This is my day."

I grumble under my breath.

"A truth for a truth?" he offers, and I motion for him to go right ahead. He chuckles, but consents to go first. "I spent an entire human lifetime here on Earth."

My eyes widen at his admission.

"Who ran Hell?"

He grunts. "The same demon who is currently threatening my reign."

"Oh, snap," I say, and his lips form a thin line.

"You sound like a human when you talk like that," he says, and I roll my eyes at his barb. "Anyway, Nolda is an idiot. He's gotten further in his quest than I thought possible, but he doesn't have the brains to carry it all the way to the end."

"If you know who it is, why haven't you dragged him back to Hell and tortured him?"

"Oh, don't you worry your pretty little head over the details. He'll have centuries of torture ahead." Luke folds his hands together, placing them on top of the yellow-checkered tablecloth. "Right now, I'm allowing him to earn every bit of his punishment."

"You're not at all concerned that a coven is helping him? Even if he isn't smart enough to bring war to your doorstep, they could."

His eyes are two impenetrable screens keeping me out of his internal thoughts as effectively as bars on a prison cell. The stony glare he directs at me has unease sweeping through me. Luke shakes his head, and the hard glower disappears.

I want to ask him what that was all about, but something tells me he's done with the conversation around witches and his demon traitor.

"Why did you decide to leave Hell for a time?" I ask, steering us back to safer pastures.

His shoulders relax, indicating he likes the new direction. "Why not?" he answers my question with one of his own, but I don't take the bait.

"Fine," he says, relenting. "Like I said before, I wanted to *feel*."

The honesty gives me pause.

"How so?" I question, not entirely understanding his reasons.

He bites out a harsh laugh. "Victoria, you know as well as I do that our father doesn't allow his children to experience what he's gifted to humans. Even when he banished me to Hell, he kept me in metaphorical chains. I could rule and cause intense emotions for others, but I myself couldn't enjoy those same pleasures. Even pain is better than feeling nothing. I just got to witness others enjoying the perks of Earth."

Wow, I thought to myself. The great devil, who governs sin and desire, wanted to feel. It was almost poetic justice that the very thing he unleashed on the world was the one thing he himself was deprived of. It was kind of sad in a sense.

"What our dear old dad forgot was that on Earth, his rules for us don't apply." A grin spread out over his face. "So I found the loophole and took a holiday."

"What did you do?"

He smirks. "Do you really want to know the dirty details, love?" he asks, but jumps right in without so much as a second for me to answer. "Drugs, booze, gambling . . . sex," he whispers, with a raised brow.

I grimace, my mind conjuring up all kids of scenarios, and he is right, I don't want any more details. He smiles at my discomfort and I glare in response. Jealousy slithers in uninvited, making my skin crawl and my fists clench and unclench under the table.

"There's no need for jealousy, love. I never cared for any of them."

"That's even worse, Lucifer. Using women isn't a sport."

"Every one of them gladly participated and knew their part in our time together," he explains. "There was so much I hadn't experienced, and they were eager to show me. I chased every high I could . . ." He takes a deep breath. "And then I saw you."

My eyes fall away from him, needing to look anywhere but at his gorgeous green eyes that threaten to pull me under his spell. I don't want to hear any more. I am about to tell him as much when he continues on.

"I wanted to know you, Victoria. I'd enjoyed so much of the time I'd spent on Earth, but that night—" He smiles to himself. "Those few minutes with you made me feel more than I had felt in all the years I'd spent here."

The weight of his admission cloaks me like a thick wool garment, threatening to pull me to the ground. I don't have

161

words. I can hardly think past all the voices in my head, screaming for me to run while I can.

"Can I get you two something to drink?" a woman croons, bringing my eyes up. She doesn't look my way at all. Her focus is solely on Luke.

He clears his throat, looking down at the menu the woman has placed in front of him.

"Excuse me," I say, as snarky as possible. "Can I get one of those too?"

"Mmmhmm," she says unintelligibly, never looking my way but nearly throwing the laminated menu at my chest.

My mouth drops open in righteous outrage. Luke covers his mouth with his own menu, stifling the smile at my reaction to the waitress's blatant flirting and outright dismissal of me.

"Do you two need a room?" I bark. Luke chokes and the bleach-blonde waitress with the gaudy mauve lipstick fans herself while mustering up an artificial look of mortification.

Luke pulls himself together, sitting taller and clearing his throat. "We'll take two Cokes and two bacon, egg, and cheese croissants to go, Marcy."

She beams in his direction, nodding enthusiastically, as though he'd given her some kind of earth-shattering praise. She saunters off, swinging her hips more than is necessary.

I scowl. "Marcy?"

He shrugs. "She was shouting it in her head, like she wanted me to know."

"Disgusting," I blurt, pulling a face that says, *I might throw up.*

I shouldn't be surprised by Marcy's reaction. The poor woman can't help herself. He is the devil, and, in all fairness, he radiates sexuality. If he can affect a fallen angel like he does, surely a poor mortal can't help herself.

I mentally slap myself for making excuses for the woman. Plenty of people turn their backs on Lucifer. Those that don't find themselves burning for eternity, and if I don't pull myself together, I might just meet that same damned fate. I don't put anything past God at this point.

DEAD INSIDE

Towering grey structures block the visitors that roam the sacred home of the dead, leaving me to feel completely alone with the devil by my side. Each and every tomb is different from the next. Many are chipped and worn to the point that even standing directly in front of one, I'm unable to read the epitaph carved into the stone.

"What are you thinking?" Luke asks, sidling up next to me.

"I wonder who this person was," I admit. "Are they in Heaven, or is one of your demons torturing them in hell?"

"Neither," he says matter-of-factly. "*She,*" he stresses, "is stuck here in purgatory. She's leaned up against that stone over there watching you rather intently," he says, pointing toward a tall mausoleum.

My nose scrunches in confusion, as I see nothing.

He chuckles. "Our girl Rosa doesn't trust you."

"Who?"

"Rosa Cortez, the deceased woman whose tomb you're loitering in front of."

"Is there any woman, living or dead, that you're not on a first name basis with?"

He spins me toward him, pulling me into his firm chest

and effectively knocking the wind right out of me. "Must we spend our one day together throwing barbs and fighting jealousy? I'm here with you. It's all that I want, Victoria."

I step out of his embrace, clearing my throat. "Twenty-four hours, Lucifer. It's all you have. I'll do my best to follow your rules, but this isn't fun for me. I'm here because you're forcing me to be."

His eyes darken, a cloud of anger rolling over his handsome features, highlighting his true nature.

Good. Be the bad guy. Make it easy for me to keep you at arm's length.

As quickly as the anger has come, it's gone. Surely, he read my mind and realized that showing his evil isn't in his best interest. The king of deceit isn't dumb. He knows how to play the game.

I walk toward the very back of the cemetery, stopping periodically to read a tombstone that catches my attention. That's when I see her.

A few tombstones ahead, luminescent and hovering above the ground, a young woman with raven black hair and haunting black eyes peers at me with a mix of interest and wariness.

A spirit.

These are not beings I'm very familiar with. I don't know their abilities or which side of the war they'd join—assuming there is a war of good versus evil.

"Rosa?" I call out, and she retreats, running even farther into the labyrinth of graves, and I follow, picking up my pace.

I weave in and out of tombs, trying desperately to catch her, but she's always one step ahead of me. Eventually, I give up, having lost sight of her. I'm bent over, breathing heavy from my chase, when I feel a rush of cold fall over my back. I turn around and freeze at the specter suspended inches from me. Her head is tilted at an odd angle, inspecting me as if I were something alien.

"What are you?" she rasps, with what can only be

described as a death rattle. "I thought you were something evil at first. You're surrounded by darkness and it chills me to be near you," she enlightens me. "It's almost as if you're dead inside."

Why do people keep saying that, and what the hell does it even mean?

"I'm perfectly alive," I say, nerves racked by her description of how she views me.

Can nobody else see her? People walk by, staring at me like I'm the strange one.

"Let me . . . touch you," she asks for permission, but moves forward without gaining it. I take a quick step back, bumping into something hard. I don't bother to look, assuming it's yet another grave marker. "I won't hurt you," she assures me, but I'm not feeling any better about the idea.

Ghosts are unnatural creatures. Once you die, you're supposed to move on. Heaven or Hell—those are your options, yet some souls remain trapped on Earth by their own choices. Luke said it's purgatory, but he and I have different views on what that entails.

As far as angels were told, purgatory is more of a state of reliving your final moments, over and over again. A sort of pre-torture. Some souls come out repentant and are allowed through the gates, while others become the worst part of themselves and are thrust into Hell.

Whatever this woman is experiencing isn't natural, and the thought of allowing her to touch me doesn't sit well. However, a larger part of me—a very moronic part—is curious what she'll find. So, I do the dumbest thing I can and step into her touch.

An icy chill creeps over me, frosting every part from my head to my toes. I fear I'll freeze if I don't move away, but I am fixed in place.

Her soulless black eyes narrow, and her lips smack irritatingly. "Your light is being eclipsed," she murmurs, more to herself than to me. "You're actually rather warm to the touch."

Funny, I think to myself. *I feel like a solid sheet of ice thanks to you.*

She lets her hand drop loosely to her side. "He's coming," she whispers.

"Who?" I say, leaning in to the spirit.

"The one who's trying to take everything from you. He won't stop until there's nothing left."

"Who?" I press, wanting her to say his name. Fearing I already know.

Without another word, she evaporates before my eyes.

"Everything all right?" Luke calls from behind me.

My eyes narrow, back turned to him. I recount the ghost's words.

What else can you take from me, Luke?

This time I know the game, and only I can allow him to take any more of me.

We've both been abnormally quiet, considering neither one of us has managed to go this long without throwing an insult or barb since Luke walked back into my life. The ghost's words haunt me still. It shouldn't come as a surprise, but a naive part of me had hoped he'd changed.

He's the devil. He's incapable of change.

I'm wondering what he is thinking about when he turns toward me, stopping us both in the middle of a crowded sidewalk. Impatient pedestrians mumble curses at us, but it doesn't faze Luke.

"What she said," he starts, then stops, looking agitated. "It's not me, Victoria. I don't wish to bring you any harm."

Someone shoves into me from behind, pushing me into Luke's firm embrace. His arms come around me, sheltering me from everyone around us. "I feel like a broken record, but

I need you to hear me, Victoria. It's *not* me you should fear. Do you believe me?"

His eyes search mine and I sigh.

"I do." My head tilts back, looking up to the sky as if someone up there will come save me from myself. "Please don't make a fool of me again, Luke."

His searing gaze doesn't leave mine when he replies, "Never again." He places a chaste kiss to the top of my head. I inhale sharply at the gesture, feeling like I could swoon.

BLOODY VALENTINE

THE FULL MOON shines down on us, casting a glow across the city. People gawk at Luke and push their way closer to him. He doesn't appear to notice as his eyes light up and a smile takes over his once serious expression. "Let's dance," he says, motioning toward a door to a club.

"Umm. No," I shake my head, walking out of his grasp. "I'm the worst dancer that ever lived."

"Let me lead. I'm *very* good," the innuendo isn't lost on me. If his words weren't sexy enough, the way his tongue darts out, running across his lower lip, does the trick of lowering my defenses.

He grabs my hand, interlacing our fingers, and drags me toward the door.

Nothing good can come of me being in the devil's arms for the night.

I allow him to lead me into what can only be described as a den of turpitude. The room is packed full of gyrating bodies, the fragrance of the place equal parts sweat and a cacophony of various perfumes and colognes. The odor is enough to gag a person. My hand comes up to shield my nose as I will my senses to adjust to the onslaught.

We take a seat at a round high-top table at the back of the

room, voyeurs to the overt displays of desire playing out like a porno in front of us. Two fallen angels attempting to not get caught up in the fray—at least I am trying not to. Lucifer, on the other hand, is basking in it. This energy fuels him like the storms do me.

I attempt to make conversation to distract me from the lovers entwined in each other. Nothing good can come from any lapse in judgment on my part. This place is sin wrapped up in a dark and musky club located in the underbelly of New Orleans. It's fitting that Lucifer would simply happen across it.

I've lived here for years, but I've never stumbled upon this place, yet there is something achingly familiar about it too. It's as though the devil himself orchestrated the entire happenstance.

Very likely.

"Thank you, Victoria," Luke says from across the table, placing his hand on top of mine.

"For what?" I ask reluctantly.

"For obliging me." He smiles. "You've been a good sport today."

I roll my eyes. "You didn't give me a choice, Lucifer."

His face falls, but just slightly.

"Please stop calling me that," he says, looking young and uncertain.

"It's your name."

He blows out a harsh breath. "Just for tonight, can I be someone else?"

The sincerity in his voice tugs at my heartstrings. Could he truly wish to be someone else? Could the side of him that I catch glimpses of be his true nature? I've spent so much time villainizing him that it's hard to switch views. It's not a stretch to imagine that even the ruler of Hell wants a break.

I consider how the request was made too; it was more of a plea than a demand. In a place like this, he's king. These people would relish walking alongside Lucifer. Yet he just wants to be anyone else.

"They're not all bad," he says, reading my mind for the millionth time. "Some of them just want to be someone else for the night. Can you blame them?"

"Are we still talking about these people? Or you?"

"Both?" He huffs. "Doesn't it ever get exhausting being this divine creature that everyone expects so much from?"

I lower my head, feeling exposed, vulnerable, under Lucifer's intense gaze. "It's been a long time since anyone has expected anything from me," I admit. I say it so quietly, he shouldn't hear it over the music, but this is Lucifer we're talking about.

"You're wrong," he says, shaking his head as though that should be the most obvious truth. "Do you really think you and that hunter of yours are the only fallen angels on Earth?"

I narrow my eyes at the direction this conversation is taking.

"Are you saying we're not?"

He laughs at me like I'm adorable, and I glare in response. "Of course you're not. The only difference is you're allowed to roam in the open. The others have to hide because if the arcs found them, they'd be exterminated."

"Why?" I press, wanting—no, needing—him to tell me everything.

For so long, I felt isolated and alone. *Until Zeke.*

"You're doing God's dirty work for him here on Earth. You fell, yet you're still working for him. You're cheap labor, and it saves his precious angels," he grinds out the words. "The others, those who fell to simply enjoy Earth's trappings . . ." He wiggles his brows, but I don't react. I want him to continue. He frowns but relents. "You serve a purpose. They don't."

"They tried to do the same to me."

"They were messing with you, and only because you insulted one of them. I didn't really need to save you, Victoria. God never would've allowed Malachi to kill you. He would've intervened if I hadn't."

"I don't think so," I say, shaking my head.

"I *know* so. You are part of a bigger picture. This war you speak of—" He stops, staring intently into my eyes. "You're right. It's coming."

There are so many questions running through my head, and I want to ask them all, but he puts his finger up and shakes it back and forth.

"This is my night, and I'm done talking about *Him*."

I bite my lip, one more question on the tip of my tongue, and I can't help but spit it out.

"Do you know why Zeke betrayed me?"

He picks at something on the table, averting my eyes. "You already know the answer to that, love."

"Was anything he said to me true?" I wish I could take the question back, so as to not sound so pathetic. Seeking validation from the devil is a recipe for disaster, and I'm feeding right into it.

He blows out an exasperated breath. "You'll have to ask him. Though why you'd bother is the greater question. He's God's pawn, Victoria. I doubt you'll get the full truth."

"I'm sorry I asked."

"The truth is hard to hear. He stole your innocence and sold you to God as a prisoner of war."

"Unreal, Luke. Why would you even need to bring that up?"

"Why not? It's true. He deflowered something that wasn't meant for him."

"Yuck. Why don't you just pee on me now?"

He raises a brow, smirking. "That sounds devilish."

"One more word and deal or no, I'll break this arrangement and take my chances in Hell."

"You know that's not exactly a threat. I want you in Hell."

I groan, snapping my attention back to the people swaying to the music.

A cover band plays on stage, the current song something new by MGK. It feels appropriate, considering Luke has dubbed tonight Valentine's Day. I chuckle at the words, so very freaking fitting.

"Dance with me," he says, standing and holding out his hand.

"Nope." I shake my head. "Like I said, I can't."

"My night. My rules. Up," he commands.

I glower back at the devil but concede, knowing that if I don't, he'll find some loophole to extend my sentence.

Luke slips right into the fray, bouncing around like every other twenty-something in the joint. He looks like he fits, his youthful features making him look no older than twenty-five. I savor the way his black tee showcases every exquisite muscle underneath. *Stop!*

He bumps his shoulder into me, the universal sign for *get your ass moving*. I roll my eyes and decide to just let go. This is his night, and I'll play the game. The atmosphere is charged, and with the low lighting and deep bass pumping below our feet, it's easy to throw caution to the wind and get lost in the fun.

It has been years since I've allowed myself to get caught up in human traditions. It seems ridiculous, considering the alleys right outside are crawling with demons. My hands come up above my head and my hips sway in time to the beat.

I have to admit it is liberating in ways not much else is. Letting go and drowning in the lyrics and bass created by the instruments is euphoric. The space is so tight that Luke takes liberties he shouldn't, constantly touching some part of me. I know I should set boundaries, but I need this night. I'm the queen of doing things for the wrong reasons, and perhaps tonight has everything to do with my need for validation. Zeke's betrayal marred a part of me that felt secure. Luke's mending those scars with every brush and every glance my way. Wrong? Probably. But I'm not going to think too much about that.

The music slows and Luke grabs both my hands in his, pulling me in and pushing me out to the beat. My eyes catch on his lips as he mouths the words to me. My stomach flips over itself, the moment so intense. So intimate. My chest swells, feeling like it could burst any moment.

The air shifts, and everything around us seems to go on. People jump around, pumping their arms in the air and bellowing the words, but in our small bubble, time freezes as if we are in a time warp and nobody else notices. We stare each other down, two starved people looking for their salvation in the other. Our bodies inch closer of their own accord, my hands coming to his chest. I lean in, closing my eyes. As if by divine intervention, the music ends and the moment is broken.

Suspended a measly inch from Luke's lips, I pull back as if he's burned me. His face pinches in something akin to pain before he takes a large step back, putting needed distance between us.

"All right guys, we're going to get karaoke started," a busty blonde on the stage calls out, signaling a changeup. "Let's give Rebel Dogs a huge round of applause for knocking us on our asses for the past hour."

Hoots and hollers rise up to levels that are uncomfortable for my celestial ears to handle. Apparently, Rebel Dogs is a favorite of everyone in the place. I have to admit, they affected me.

No. Luke affected me. Too much.

"Okay," I call out above the noise to Luke. "We've had enough of pretending to be young."

"And human," Luke smirks.

"Yeah, that too."

We're heading toward the door when the busty blonde from the stage steps into our path, bypassing me and placing a red painted nail to Luke's chest.

You've got to be kidding me.

Can this man go anywhere without drawing unnecessary attention?

Peeking a glance at them, I groan. He's laying on the charm, thick and convincingly.

The blonde is eating out of his hands. I don't even want to know what's being said. She's practically panting, and his head's thrown back, laughing at something she said. He's not even engineering her reaction to him. This is one hundred percent her reaction to his natural charm.

The blonde looks over her shoulder, leveling me with a fierce glare. I give it right back, mumbling under my breath about tramps and bar whores, when she turns toward me.

"You can't leave until one of you sings, and he says you're up."

I scrunch my nose. "Not happening."

"Come now, Victoria. Take one for the team. You owe me." He grins a slow, joker-wide smile.

I step toward him, leaning into his ear. "I can't, Lucifer. I suck at singing. Angelic voice, I have not," I admit.

He laughs. "Well, you'll have to make a trade."

My hands come to my hips and I drill him with a look that says, *you're pushing your damn luck.*

"Those are my terms," he says with a shrug.

"I'll share my bed with you."

He lifts a brow. "That's already been settled, love. You'll have to do better."

I huff, "Fine. Breakfast tomorrow. That's my final offer."

He nods. "Done."

"It seems like I'll be taking one for the team." He smiles down at the blonde, and she squeals in delight.

"What are you singing?" She claps her hands excitedly.

He puckers his lips, seemingly contemplating his choices. "'Riptide.' Vance Joy."

She nods and runs off toward the stage.

I widen my eyes to say *what the hell.* He just shrugs.

This night has been so utterly against everything I stand for. I don't relax. I don't dance. I sure as hell don't pretend to be human. Yet I can't deny that I've enjoyed every damn minute of it.

CHOP SUEY!

THE MUSIC STARTS and my eyes pop to the stage, where Luke stands at the microphone. I know exactly what to expect. He's sung to me before, on our first full night together. His voice is sultry and masculine. Every girl is about to lose her mind in a minute.

He croons into the microphone, and just as expected, there's a collective sigh from every female in the room. It doesn't help that he plays right into it, making each of them feel as though he's singing directly to them. The devil has skills, and one of his best is the way he can make you feel like you're the only person in the room.

The very reason I fell for him.

A dark part of me is eating up the way that everyone, even many of the men, are falling all over themselves to get closer to him, yet it's me he's here with. I don't deny that makes me one very disturbed girl. I'd love to say it's an aftereffect still plaguing me from our time together before, but a voice deep within chastises me for pushing the blame all on him. Some inner part of me knows that not every feeling I've felt for Luke was contrived by him. None of them were, if he's to be believed.

His soulful green eyes find mine. He smiles, never again

removing his gaze from me, singing every word straight to my heart. I feel dizzy at the proclamations, even if they're someone else's creation. I can't help but wish that each lyric sung was chosen by him for me. That he truly means every word. Foolish girl.

I internally berate myself for allowing such thoughts to infiltrate my mind, yet no matter how much I try in this moment to change my feelings, they can't be helped. Simply listening to his voice has my knees quaking, threatening to buckle underneath me. My body feels electrified, a feeling similar to when I recharge. Every synapse is firing on all cylinders, and it feels euphoric.

For the first time in a very long time, I'm content. I don't want to be anywhere else, with anyone else. All thoughts of my past and Zeke float away, until my head is clear and Luke is all I see.

When the song ends, people cheer and call for him to sing another. He lifts his hands, trying to decline, but the crowd won't allow it.

I smother my smirk with my hand at the look of distress plastered on his handsome face. He wants to be with me. I know it, and I love the feelings that simple truth sparks in me.

"All right," he says, laughing. "What'll it be?" he calls out for requests.

I don't know what the hell possesses me, but I yell out, "Broken." He doesn't need me to elaborate; he smiles a smile just for me and nods his head. The DJ gets it ready and before long, the music starts back up. Everyone around me gets into it, and before long, women are high-fiving me for my choice. He sang this song to me the last time we were together. The words spoke to my heart then, just as they do now. The memories make me smile.

My body sways on its own to the beat of the music. I soak in every sound. Every word he sings. Every. Single. Moment. As though this will be the last time. The thought is an effective dose of cold water, waking me from my fantasy and bringing me back to my sad reality. One in which I'm a fallen angel and the man I'm in love with is the devil himself.

My thoughts continue to wander down a dead-end path that only leads to devastation and betrayal. I recall the end of the last night we were together. All the unspoken truths and lies coming to a head. The crushing of my soul when he left me alone in that alley.

My face falls at the reminder of that night, the heat I felt moments ago being drowned out by bitter cold. My stomach turns and the need to flee overwhelms me. My eyes never waver from the stage. From him.

He doesn't miss the change, a deep frown marring his beautiful face. I take a few steps backward, bumping into people as I go.

"Hey!" a woman yells. I turn, wide-eyed, to apologize, but her scowl tells me she'll have none of it. Her purple hair is teased to create a dome on top of her head, and the white tank top she wears is two sizes too small for her busty chest. It's only amplified when she crosses her arms over her breasts, lifting the globes to peak out the top, showing far too much.

Words never come, as someone's shoulder smacks into mine, knocking me back a step.

My body spins, eyes connecting with Luke, who notices my obvious distress. He attempts to leave the stage, but a muscular bouncer blocks the way. He turns, leaping from the front of the platform, dropping the mic in the process. My hands fly to my ears to drown out the piercing screech it causes as I make a run for the door.

I don't want him to catch me. I need space, which is something he won't give. He's all-consuming. Smothering. And right now, it'll only lead to a fight. One in which the possibility of outing myself to humans is high, because my emotions are all over the place.

I rush from the bar, not looking back for fear he'd somehow convince me to forget my feelings and bend to his will. He wouldn't need persuasion or any other tactic. Luke is my kryptonite all on his own. I cave with a simple glance from him. He's my undoing. Has been for years.

As I'm pushing my way out the door, it hits me. This place feels familiar because it's the exact bar we'd been in that night. He was recreating our whole first date. It worked to remind me of how incredible he makes me feel, just like the last time. But everything good from that night will always be overshadowed by the way it ended. The way it's falling apart now.

Here in this place, where I'm currently ducking into safety. It's the one spot that holds the worst memories of my entire existence. The alley from the night I realized that Luke and Satan were one and the same. That what I wanted, could never be.

Why was he trying to recreate that night? To hurt me all over again? To break me once and for all? Well, it's working. Nothing about this is all right. It's cruel.

A group of demons already haunt the shadows of this place, likely summoned to this location by the proximity of their master. They move into the moonlit alley, sizing me up, as I do the same. I don't have Solis, but my anger fuels my every move. I raise my hand to create a barrier, so no human walks into this fight.

One decides to approach, and I don't waste time getting this slaughter started. Taking several steps forward, I leap into the air, spinning and kicking my leg out to send the nearest demon hurling into the stone wall. It doesn't faze him as he shakes it off and limps my way. I stalk toward him, reaching out and grabbing his head in my hands, twisting it from his shoulders, and dropping it to the ground. I continue my savage assault of the evil creatures, showing no mercy. It's not like I ever do, but my savagery is fueled by something otherworldly tonight. Something I can't control. Rage unlike anything I've ever felt consumes me.

More demons crawl out of the shadows, but none move toward me. I survey the area and find a broken pallet with jagged wood, making a perfect stake. Without taking my eyes off the creatures, I back up, bending down and breaking off the pointy piece, curling it into my palm. It's not Solis, but it'll have to do.

Coming to a stand, I size up my opponents. They're not Hell's finest, that's for sure. One step up from barnyard pigs, they're all snort and no bite. They don't even have the size advantage. These scrawny bottom feeders will be easy to take out.

"You're first," I say, pointing the wood at the nearest snout-nosed swine.

He grunts, nodding his head in my direction to his two companions. All three rush me and I nearly roll my eyes at their slow advance. When the first makes it to me, I lift onto my toes, swinging my leg around to kick him in the head and throw him back into the second demon. To finish off the last of them, I spin, sending my elbow flying back into his face.

The sound of his splitting nose would make most queasy, but I don't even flinch. I spin back around, lodging the makeshift stake into his chest. Black blood oozes from the open wound. I step back, giving myself enough space to send my foot sailing into the stake, driving it further into his chest cavity, while also sending him flying backward into the shadows from which he came.

I'm on an emotional rollercoaster, slipping from fury to sadness. My mind and heart war between kicking the shit out of the rest of these demons or lying down and allowing them to finish me. Perhaps in death, there will be peace.

Out of the corner of my eye I see another approaching. I swirl around to find a demon that looks more like a demented clown, with his Cheshire-cat smile and long pointed teeth, headed my way. He's like something out of a Stephen King novel, and that snaps me out of my momentary pity party.

My nose scrunches in disgust as he licks his lips as though he's about to make a meal out of me. I summon the last bit of energy I can and deliver two punches to the face and a knee to the groin. The demon falls to his knees, and I don't waste time twisting his head off his shoulders.

I hunch over, gasping for breath. My breathing is ragged, and all my energy spent, but more demons slink into the alley. I watch as they close in on all sides, outnumbering me. Wolves, vampires, low demons and upper echelon, all file into the alley way. My head swivels, taking in the sheer number of demons surrounding me. Never in my life have I been this overwhelmed by a horde; this is even too much for me.

What have I gotten myself into? Was this a trap set by Luke? Could he really have done this to me? My mind plays with my heart, trying to whisper conspiracy theories and traitorous allegations, painting Luke in a light worse than ever before.

No. This wasn't him.

It doesn't matter that he's Satan. Not a part of me believes this was his doing. No matter the hefty list of transgressions against him, I believe he cares. It might be a foolish dream, but it's one I intend to cling to if this is to be the end of my existence.

Straightening on wobbly, exhausted limbs, I play at bravery and motion for the next demon to approach. One at the front sniffs the air before tipping his head toward the sky and howling. He doesn't look like a wolf, but he's calling out to someone like I've witnessed the wolf-demons do. None of the others so much as flinch.

If he's calling for more, I'm as good as dead. If he's calling for Lucifer, maybe he'll spare me. With the numbers I'm currently facing, death is likely if help doesn't arrive from Heaven or Luke.

While the demon is preoccupied, I close my eyes and call to the earth, putting all my thoughts into creating a storm. A bolt of lightning likely isn't enough to save me, but I must try. If my reason for being on this earth is to kill every demon I encounter, then I will go out doing just that.

After what feels like minutes, but is likely seconds, thunder rolls through the sky, shaking the ground with its power. Several demons howl, but still, none of them make a move. Lightning streaks across the sky, lighting up the alley, showing me every single creature I'm to face before shrouding most of them back into darkness.

My hands lift into the air as I summon the sky to produce the energy I'll need. It delivers, sending a bolt of lightning straight down, burrowing into the ground at my feet. The energy spiders out, crawling up my legs and wrapping around my body, all the way to my fingertips.

I relish its caress, marveling at the way it fills me. My powers might not be fully restored, but the earth has provided, giving me a fighting chance. A sense of peace washes over me and no matter what's to come, I'm ready for it.

Taking a deep breath, I look the demon in charge directly in the eye and declare war.

"My name is Victoria. I'm a fallen angel of the second highest order of God."

A resounding growl—that shakes the area more than the thunder did—bounces off the walls of the alley, sending chills racing up my spine, but I don't recoil. Instead, I forge on.

"I choose to fight for Heaven's army, despite my circumstances. It's my promise that none of you will leave this alley while there's still breath in my lungs."

The last word is barely spoken before the horde of demons rush into battle. I crouch down, readying for impact, sending up a prayer to God as a last Hail Mary.

No more do I call out to God than he answers. At my back I feel Solis. He's delivered me salvation. I pull the sword from my back and lash out, lobbing two vampires' heads clean off their bodies in one swipe. I twist and stab, duck and deliver blow after blow, as more vampires and low-level demons fall, but it's not enough.

They're crawling out of the shadows from every angle. Either there's a portal from Hell somewhere in this alley or witch magic is at play. Nolda is likely nearby.

I can't keep up and my restored energy is near zapped already. Sweat beads down my temples as I twist to take out another, only to be met with a fist to the side of the head, causing my vision to swim. I fall to my knees, cradling my head, when another strike to the head jerks me backward.

Solis slipped from my hands at the first impact to my head. Without it, I'm doomed. On my knees I peer through blurry vision, trying and failing to locate my sword, to no avail. When all seems lost, I curl into the fetal position, not wanting to see what's coming. I never envisioned what eternal death would be like, but I sure as hell know I don't want to see my murderers coming. Maybe that makes me a coward, but I'd like to think of it as self-preservation.

I'm kicked repeatedly as I wait for what's to be the killing blow, but it never comes. The assault stops abruptly, but I don't dare open my eyes. A high-pitched wail reverberates off the ground, following by the flapping of wings. Archangels? My eyes flutter open to see what's creating the noises and stopped the demons' attack.

Aid from God—in the form of angels—didn't come, but a black knight falls from the sky, raven wings extended. He lands with one knee on the ground in front of me, and every demon retreats. Lucifer growls something in a language I don't understand, and every demon still alive scatters.

Once the realization that Luke has saved me hits, I break.

HELIUM

I KNEEL IN THE ALLEY, vanquished demons at my feet, blood everywhere. Soon they'll evaporate, but in this moment, as the adrenaline overtakes my body, it's all too much. I feel his presence behind me, and I cry out.

"Why?" I scream, emotion overtaking me.

"I'll always save you."

"No," I snap. "Why would you bring me back here? Why can't you leave that night in the past where it belongs?"

He may have saved me, but he's the reason I'm here in the first place. I fell because of his tricks. If I face him now, one of us won't make it out of this alley alive. Despite being immortal, our earthly lives can end, and not being allowed in Heaven means going to Hell. That's the one place I won't go.

"I won't allow that to happen to you," he says, reading my mind.

I laugh darkly. "You think I trust a word you say? You've done nothing but deceive me at every turn."

"Never, Victoria. I've never been untruthful with you."

My head snaps up. Our eyes collide and I put all the emotion swirling through me into my next few words.

"You left me," I snarl through my teeth.

His head falls with a sigh. "That night I made a choice

that haunts me to this day. I left you because that's what I thought you wanted."

"I did," I seethe.

"We both know that's not true. You can lie to yourself, Victoria, but you can't lie to me. I left you thinking I'd deceived you into falling." His hand runs back through his hair, pulling at the roots in apparent frustration. "All these years I've allowed what we had to be spoiled by miscommunications and my own fears."

"You're the devil, Luke. You fear nothing."

"Victoria, stand," he commands, but I stay kneeling, tears streaming down my face. He falls to his knees in front of me, hand coming under my chin to lift my head, so we're once again staring into each other's eyes. "With you I fear everything." He bites the last word. "I fear how deeply I care for you. You're here because you feel everything I do. Admit it."

"Stop," I whisper.

"No amount of time with you will be enough. I want forever. Every touch. Every kiss. Every damn night. I want you, and I know you feel the same."

"Stop," I yell, both hands grabbing at either side of my head, pulling at the roots of my hair. "Just stop. Find someone else to toy with. I'm through with these games."

His hands are on the backs of my elbows, and I jerk away, standing to my feet. Taking a deep breath, I turn to him, and my breath hitches. The king of deception stands before me looking at me like a broken man. *Master manipulator. Deceiver of man and angel.* I want nothing more than to lash out and hurt him as much as he has me. His beauty, even in this moment, has me breathless. I hate him, but I hate myself more.

"Victoria, I'm here. I've continued to save you. How do you not see how much I care? Even now you doubt me?"

His words soften my anger but manage to make me feel worse. I'm being irrational, but having a near-death experience will do that to even an angel, fallen or otherwise.

A single tear slips down my cheek, and he steps forward,

wiping it away. His touch burns my skin, lighting me on fire from the inside out. It's a painful reminder that I'll never feel this for anyone else. The devil himself is the only one who can elicit such feelings.

"Please," I beg. "Don't do this to me."

"Victoria, it's you who's killing me slowly. You've turned my life upside down. You make me want to throw everything away because I can't get you out of my head. You're all I see. All I think about. I can't stay away."

"Lies," I say weakly. I can fight this pull all I want, but I know what he says is true. I feel it in every inch of my being. My soul calls out to him and I'm a fool to resist. There is no resisting when I know I feel the same.

I'm in love. I have been from the beginning.

"No lies, beautiful." He moves a piece of hair out of my eyes, placing it behind my ear. "I'm in love with you."

My breath hitches.

"Don't say such things."

"I'll say it, because I mean every damn word."

He pulls me in to him, crashing his lips to mine as rain pours down over us and lightning flashes overhead. The thunder our kiss creates sends goose bumps racing over my skin. I'm lost to the sensations coursing through me. I want to get lost in his touch, give myself to the dark side so it never ends. His hands run down my back, continuing the onslaught of sensation. When he pulls away, I whimper, feeling the loss immediately. His forehead rests against mine.

"Come with me. Stand by my side," Luke begs, sounding like a desperate man.

"I—Luke . . ." The words are stuck in my throat. I want to give in. I want to hand my life over to him. But the words won't come out.

"Victoria, don't run away."

I take a step back, eyes never leaving his. Pain, fear . . . love is reflected back at me, and it's my undoing.

"I love you, Luke. I always have. But I can't force myself to be something I'm not. I can't rule Hell. No matter how I feel about you, we can never be."

"Then I'll relinquish my throne. I'll live with you here, on Earth."

He's so serious it breaks my heart. Does he not realize that it's an impossible promise to keep? It's one he has no control over, because it's not just his decision.

"You and I both know Heaven won't allow it, Luke."

"Then I'll go to war."

My hand rests against his cheek, caressing his soft skin. "I won't let you."

"Tori?" Zeke's voice pulls me out of the moment. What the hell is he doing here?

I whip around to see Zeke's ashen face and fallen expression. As if he has any right to feel anything about what he's just witnessed.

"What are you doing here?" Luke growls, but Zeke doesn't pay any attention to him.

He steps forward as though he's going to take Zeke on, but my hand shoots to his chest, stopping his advance.

"Let me handle this. Please."

Luke scowls but nods his agreement. I turn back toward Zeke.

He takes a step forward but remains in the shadows.

"I tracked you, Tori. We need to talk."

"Like hell I'm allowing you near her," Luke warns, voice menacing.

I turn my head toward him, placing both hands on his chest. "Please. Give me a minute. I only have a few things to say to him, but they need to be said. Will you allow me just that?"

Luke grinds his teeth and blows air out from his nostrils. It's clear he doesn't like this.

"Victoria—"

"Please, Luke." I cut him off, done asking for permission.

This is my life, and if Luke wants any part of it, he'll understand that this is important to me.

He groans. "Fine. But you don't leave my sight. Do you understand?"

I nod.

"Something doesn't feel right, Victoria."

"He's angry. Either he knows I know his secrets, or he's furious because he just caught me in your arms."

"That's what I'm afraid of. What is he capable of if he knows his secret's out?"

I smirk. "I can take him. Trust me."

He groans. "Make it fast."

I head toward Zeke at the end of the alley, and the closer I get, the more uncomfortable I grow. Something is off with Zeke. His stance, the way his hands are pushed into the pockets of his jeans—all of his mannerisms are off. Maybe Luke is right. He might be unhinged and dangerous.

"Tori," he sneers. "I see you've been sneaking around with Satan. Now you're his whore too?"

I jerk back. His voice. His words. Nothing is right about him.

I turn toward Luke, ready to call for help, but it never happens. Before I'm able to say a word or Lucifer is able to react to my distress, I'm scooped up into Zeke's arms and everything goes black.

Want to know how Tori's story ends? Grab **Trust the Fall!** Available now!

BOOKS BY MELISSA WINTERS

Blood Legends

Click to purchase

Blood That Binds

Blood That Reigns

Blood That Burns

Blood That Serves

Fallen Hunters

Fear the Fall

Trust the Fall

The Pandora Chronicles

Secrets Legends Keep

Lies Legends Tell

MEET MELISSA

Melissa Winters' debut novel, Blood That Binds, has been in the works since 2009. She finally mustered up the courage to push publish, and now she's sitting back and biting her nails—which is one of her many bad habits. Writing and coffee keep her sane, but have also contributed to her being nocturnal! All things paranormal and witchy excite her. She hates to cook and work out, but will suck it up if it means one more hour to listen to whatever audiobook is currently on queue.

Melissa lives in the suburbs of Cincinnati with her husband, three kids and dog.

Keep up to date with my new releases and sales ➜ https://melissaholtz.com/newsletter/

Printed in Great Britain
by Amazon